REMINISCE MYSTERIES
BOOK 1

Reminisce line of books by Kirk House Publishers

For Mom

My beautiful mother Mary

REMINISCE MYSTERIES
BOOK 1

Stories on the Mysterious Side

A Collection of Stories by Kirk House Publishers

Reminisce Mysteries – Book 1
Stories on the Mysterious Side
Copyright © 2022 by Kirk House Publishers

First Edition
978-1-952976-80-3 paperback
978-1-952976-81-0 eBook
978-1-952976-82-7 hardcover
Library of Congress Control Number: 2022940945

Cover and Interior Design by Ann Aubitz
Images from Book Brush and Adobe Stock

Published by Kirk House Publishers
1250 E 115th Street
Burnsville, MN 55337
Kirkhousepublishers.com
612-781-2815

FOREWORD

When Ann Aubitz from Kirk House Publishers called me about the new line of books she was publishing for older readers, my ears perked up. I knew this was an underserved market. Ann explained her series would be different from the books currently available. Her books were actually inspired by an elder, her 96-year-old mother, who still enjoys reading.

I was excited to review the books myself, as so often books for our elders have small print, they are hard to hold, or have storylines that are too complicated to comprehend, or on the other side, they are overly simplified and child-like.

What I found was Ann's books (the Reminisce book line) were designed to be dignified and intriguing. In addition, they would meet multiple needs:

1. Large print for older eyes.
2. The Larger-sized book makes it easier to hold as it is common for fine motor skills to decline as we age.
3. Intriguing storylines for all ages. This allows flexibility to share intergenerationally, allowing grandma or grandpa to read to their grandchildren, or their grandkids can read the book to their grandparents; if they are in the mood to share.
4. Along the lines of intergenerational, the books also can teach children a bit about the past and engage in conversation about the good old days that elders refer to.
5. These books are ideal for a wide range of people and abilities of various ages, and for those with early cognition issues, they are IDEAL!

The stories are set in the 1940s, 1950s, and 1960s in an easy-to-read, short-story format in the genres we love, mystery, romance, ghost stories, and science fiction. Large type and full-colored illustrations make the stories accessible to all readers, many of whom may have their own special memories of those periods of history.

This series will meet a wide range of needs, enabling many people who love to read to continue having that pleasure.

I highly recommend the Reminisce book line for your special someone that still loves to read.

~Lori La Bey, founder of Alzheimer's Speaks

Alzheimer's Speaks is a Minnesota-based advocacy group and media outlet making an international impact. Our goal is to shift dementia care from crisis to comfort by giving voice to all and raising those voices to enrich lives by sharing critical information, personal stories, resources, products, and tools from people and organizations at all levels around the world.

Website: https://alzheimersspeaks.com

TABLE OF CONTENTS

INTRODUCTION

When I was young, the greatest joy for me was reading books. But, of course, this was before reading was cool like it is now. It was a time when my friends were playing their first computer games, but not me—my nose was always buried in a book. In those stories, I went to far-off places and had amazing adventures. In those stories, I could be free.

I credit my love of reading to my mom. Born in 1926 to a family with sixteen children, she never finished high school, but she had a thirst for knowledge and reading that thrived throughout the years.

I remember only a few times while growing up that my mom didn't have a book, magazine, or word puzzle in her hands—she had an insatiable quest for knowledge.

In her Senior Living facility library, she discovered a book that she loved. It was *Little Women* by American novelist

Louisa May Alcott. It was altered from the original book in a good way. This book contained illustrations and larger print. My mom would run her fingers over the pictures to remember a time long past. She read and reread the book.

Unfortunately for her, there were no other books like this in the library. She tried and failed to read books with more complex storylines and smaller type. She would get frustrated and distraught because reading no longer brought her joy.

This is why I started this line of books. It is for people like me and my mom that LOVE to read. These books are meant to be easy to read, have a complete storyline, and help readers remember a time long past and *to reminisce*.

Kirk House Publishers is proud to present the Reminisce Line of reader-friendly books. Written by several authors, the stories are set in the 1940s, 1950s, and 1960s in an easy-to-read, short-story format. Large type and full-colored illustrations make the stories accessible to all readers, many of whom may have their own special memories of those periods of history.

Happy Reading!

~Ann Aubitz

THE DEADLY DANCE
By Ann Aubitz

"Come on, Rhonda, don't be like that. Let me give you a ride home."

"I don't wanna ride home from you, Jack."

"Oh, come on, just get in. Isn't it a beauty? And only three miles on her! Let's burn rubber and show 'em what this car can do! I got her for a real steal at the car lot today—it's a 1955 Ford Thunderbird."

"I don't care what it is, Jack. I know the car really razzes your berries, but I don't wanna ride from you. I don't want anything from you."

"Why you gotta be like that? You know I didn't mean anything by it."

"You just announced to all our friends that we were engaged. Well, I don't remember no ring."

"Well, we're as good as engaged. And I'll get your stinking ring. So, what's wrong with telling our friends?"

"Because it's not true, Jack. I never agreed to marry you. I wanna get out of this town and live my life. Nothing exciting ever happens here."

"And you can't live your life with me? We'd rule this town—we'd have it made in the shade. I thought I meant something to you."

"You do mean something to me, Jack—you're my friend. You've been my friend forever. But I can't believe you embarrassed me like that. What were you thinking?"

"I was thinking I want to marry you."

"Huh. No, you were thinking that you would be a big buttinsky with my dance with Thomas."

"What do you see in that city slicker anyway?"

"I see a nice handsome man who asked me to dance."

"You can't fool me. You see him as your ticket out of this place."

"What's so wrong with that, Jack? What's wrong with wanting more for my life than this town has to offer?"

"It's wrong if you run off with the first guy who asks you to dance. You're only eighteen, for Christ's sake. So what's your hurry?"

"What's my hurry. What's *your* hurry? You just told everyone we were getting married."

The night had been so amazing, except for this conversation. It was magical: the music, the dancers, the poodle skirts swinging in the air, around the floor in delicious colors. It was the first dance Rhoda was able to attend without her parents since turning eighteen.

Rhonda smelled smoke and realized they weren't alone in the parking lot. A man in a trench coat stood in a dark corner smoking a cigarette; she watched him, then reluctantly got in Jack's car. She took a deep breath and inhaled the new car smell. They rode in silence the two miles to her house, and she jumped out of the car before Jack had a chance to say anything. As Rhonda walked into the house, her father walked out to take a look at Jack's new Thunderbird.

Much later that night...

"Jack Thompson, open the door! It's the Dayton police," the policeman yelled as he pounded on the door.

"I'm coming, Bobby. What's this Dayton police shit? And why are you at my pad at three o'clock in the morning?" Jack swung open the door to the only two officers on the Dayton police force, and he counted at least three of the sheriff's deputies standing on his front porch.

"What's going on, Bobby?"

Instead of answering his question, he said, "Jack Thompson, you are under arrest for the murder of Thomas Griffon."

"What? Bobby, this isn't funny. If you want to stay over, get rid of your buddies and come in."

"This is no joke, Jack. Thomas Griffon was found murdered in the Dayton County Dance Hall parking lot, just hours after you were witnessed having an altercation with him."

"Bobby, stop talking gibberish and using big words like *altercations*. We did not fight; I never laid a finger on him. Now, if you excuse me, I am going back to sleep. I have to work in the morning." Jack started shutting the door and turning away. As soon as he did, all five officers rushed at him and pinned him to the floor.

"Bobby don't be a wet rag. We've been friends since we were in diapers."

"Sorry, Jack, gotta bring you in. Some witnesses saw you stewing because your girl was dancing with the victim."

One of the older deputies was losing his patience. "Officer, get the suspect detained and get him in the car. We will sort this out at the precinct."

The next day, Rhonda walked into Rusty's Malt Shop and scanned the area for her friend.

"Hey, Rhonda, over here!" Suzie waved as she slid over on the cushioned red leather booth to make room.

Before she could even get her butt on the seat, Suzie started gibbering. "Hey, Rhonda, did you hear that that city slicker Thomas was murdered last night in the parking lot at the dance hall?"

"No way... You mean the guy I danced with is dead? That's terrible."

"Umm, there's something else I should tell you."

"Well, what is it, Suzie. Spit it out."

"The police arrested Jack for his murder."

"My Jack? Are you sure, Suzie?"

Rhonda loved Suzie like a sister, but she was a little truth-challenged at times.

"Your Jack, huh. Last night you had your undies in a twist because he said you were engaged."

"I was just surprised, is all."

"Well, you seemed more than surprised. You were mad as a hornet."

"I need to go see him now," Rhonda said, sliding out of the booth.

"What do you mean now? We haven't had lunch yet."

"Sorry, Suzie, I gotta get to Jack."

Rhonda knew in her heart it couldn't be Jack. Jack would never kill anyone. She ran to the police station, her saddle shoes clicking on the pavement.

She burst into the building huffing and puffing and stopped at the front desk.

"Bobby, I need to see Jack right now."

"Rhonda, I don't think it's a good idea that you are here. Jack is in a pile of trouble."

"Bobby, you know darn well that Jack didn't kill Thomas. Let me see him right now or I'll call your mamma."

Bobby shook his head. "Fine, Rhonda, I will take you in to see him now, but just for a minute. You hear me?"

"Whatever you say, daddy-o!" She gave him a mock salute and followed him down to the holding cells.

"Jack, you have a visitor, but just for a short visit, you understand?"

Jack ignored Bobby and instead watched Rhonda walk into the room and stand across from him on the other side of the bars.

"Rhonda, what are you doing here? I don't want you to see me like this."

"Jack, I know you didn't do this, and I can prove it."

"What? How can you prove this? Rhonda, you're just a kid." Bobby said.

"For your information, Bobby, I turned eighteen last week, so I am not a kid anymore. Let me tell you how I can prove it."

Rhonda swung around so she was facing both men.

"Word from the bird Bobby, Jack couldn't have done it because he drove me home before midnight. My daddy came out to admire his new car, so he didn't leave until twelve thirty."

"See right there, Rhonda, you don't know what you're talking about. Jack could've dropped you off and gone back to finish off Thomas. The coroner estimates the time of death at 1:00 a.m. So, you see, Jack had plenty of time to drive the two miles back to the dance hall, kill the victim, and then return home with no one the wiser."

Rhonda huffed and blew her bangs off her forehead. Then she smiled and said to Bobby, "Did you check the odometer on his car?"

"What? No, why would we have done that?"

"Because if you checked his odometer, you would know that he never went back to the dance hall. When he bought the car yesterday, there were only three miles on it. Jack drove straight to the dance hall after picking the car up. He dropped me off and drove home. So you should be able to calculate the miles."

Bobby looked stunned, and Jack had a big smile on his face.

"Well, by God, you did figure it out. But I still have to verify the miles on your car, Jack, and if it adds up, I am very sorry for all of this."

Bobby ran out of the room to verify this latest information.

Rhonda turned and smiled at Jack, feeling very happy she knew him.

"And you said nothing exciting ever happens in this town." Jack smiled.

Bobby came back and said everything was copacetic and Jack could leave the station with Rhonda. On the way back to Rusty's, they talked about their future in the small town they called home.

Later that day, the sheriff's men picked up two men crossing the Minnesota state line in a stolen car with the murder weapon in the backseat.

It turned out that Thomas was a con artist who got on the bad side of the wrong person and was shot and killed in their small town where nothing exciting ever happens.

ABOUT THE AUTHOR

Ann Aubitz is the Co-owner and Publisher of Kirk House Publishers and FuzionPress, located in Burnsville, Minnesota. After years of reading everything she could get her hands on, she decided to help others achieve their dream of becoming an author. Her mission is to help authors reach their goals by seeing their books in print.

Ann is also a proud member of the Independent Book Publishers Association, a Board Member-At-Large for the Midwest Independent Publishers Association, and a group leader for Women of Words and chairs the yearly WOW writing conference.

STORY TWO
ERNIE'S TREASURE
By Addison Frost

Maggie flipped the sign on the door to "CLOSED" the same way she had done every day since she was a kid working at her father's bakery. She felt like someone was watching her, so she looked out the window but didn't see a soul outside the bakery at this time of night.

As she felt the cold steel of the sign in her hand, she hoped she would get the opportunity to flip the sign to "OPEN" again.

She had cause for concern—her father Ernie had passed away a few days ago. He'd been in perfect health, or so she thought. But unfortunately, he suffered from a heart attack at the age of forty-seven.

The last few days had been some of the hardest of Maggie's life. Not just because her dad died but because no one could find her father's will. The bakery's future hung in the balance.

She knew in her heart that he had left all his worldly possessions to her. She was his only child, and her mom had passed away many years ago.

So she was all he had left—well, she and the bakery and the tiny apartment they shared. She vowed to continue in his tradition of running the bakery in this little Chicago suburb.

The payphone rang, pulling Maggie from her thoughts. Maggie picked up the receiver and heard a nasally voice. "Operator, do you accept a collect call from Judy Dresser?"

"Yes, Olive, I accept the charges."

"Thanks, Maggie, I will put her through. You girls have a good chat now, and Maggie, I am so sorry to hear about your pa. If you need anything, just let me know."

"Ummm, thanks again, Olive." Maggie was never sure how to respond to people these days.

"Hey Judy, how are you?"

"Oh Maggie, honey, I am fine. How are you doing? I am so sorry I couldn't get back for your dad's funeral today."

"I know, Judy, it's okay. He would have understood."

"He was so patient with me and my wild ways."

"Oh Judy, he loved you like a daughter."

"That's why I am so sorry that I can't be there for you."

"You've called every day since it happened to check in on me. It's almost like you're here with me."

"The phone is the best invention ever, right Maggie? I can't remember what we ever did without it." Judy paused, "So, I hate to ask, but did you find it?"

"No, I've looked, but I can't find his will anywhere."

"What happens if you don't find it?"

"Then the bakery, the apartment, and everything he owned will revert to the bank."

"You know his ex-partner Bradley would just love for that to happen. He has been waiting to get his grimy hands on the bakery for years.

"I know, Judy, and I will be heartbroken if that happens."

"I will be home tomorrow to help you look for it. We will find it, I promise you."

Maggie finished the call and closed out the register for the day.

Another busy day. They had been doing a great business in the neighborhood ever since Ernie got rid of his no-good

partner Bradley. A few years ago, Ernie had noticed something was wrong. He couldn't figure out why they were so busy all the time but not making any money. Then he figured it out—Bradley had been skimming money from the till before he made the bank deposits.

The thing is that Ernie wouldn't press charges. Bradley was one of his best friends from childhood, and he couldn't bear to have him rot in jail. So he forgave him and dissolved their arrangement. But Bradley never forgave Maggie's dad. So ever since, Bradley had vowed to put Ernie out of business.

Later that night, Maggie sat upright in her bed. Her dream startled her awake. It was so vivid it almost seemed real.

It was a dream about her dad. They were playing like they always did on Saturday mornings. It was the only day of the week that Ernie opened the shop late. He wanted to spend the morning with Maggie. In her dream, her dad turned to her as she played with one of the wooden puzzles and said, "You can find it, Maggie. I believe in you." Then she awoke.

Some of the fondest memories of her dad were when they would play games and put together puzzles. "Puzzles are good for the mind," her dad would always say. Then he would pull out giant jigsaw puzzles and wooden hidden passage puzzles.

They had the WWII puzzles, Daniel Boone, Howdy Doodie, and so many more. Each time a new puzzle would come out, Ernie would have to buy it. He had no bad habits like smoking or drinking but did have an obsession with puzzles. When he left the house, he almost always came back with a puzzle in his hand.

The wooden hidden passage puzzles were different; Ernie made them himself. They were made of twelve or more wooden pieces that he had hand-carved and fit together in a way that very few people were able to crack. The only people who could solve the puzzles were Maggie, Judy, and of course, Ernie.

Some people, like Bradley, thought that the puzzles were a waste of time. He didn't like that Ernie closed the shop on

Saturday morning when that could have been a big revenue day for them. But Ernie insisted. Maggie thought Bradley's distaste for puzzles came from the fact that he never solved one. It would infuriate him to consider that anyone, especially Maggie, was more intelligent than him.

Maggie smiled as she got out of bed. It was like her father was there with her. She turned to look at the clock, and it was only three in the morning. Not quite time to start baking for the day. She had about an hour to look through the puzzles and see if she could find anything. It would be just like her father to leave her a clue in a puzzle to find his will.

Maggie hurried and got dressed. She went into their living room, which had doubled as the game room as a child. They would spread the puzzles on the floor when she was small and go through them until they were all solved. When they started getting too easy for Maggie, Ernie made more difficult wooden ones with more pieces and sliding hidden compartments.

That's it! Maggie slapped herself on the forehead. So that must be where he hid a clue where the will was stashed.

Maggie grabbed all the wooden puzzles from their resting places on the shelves. There were at least fifty of them that she had to solve—and quickly. She knew that the bank owner would start working on her dad's case in a day to two. Although they had already contacted the local lawyer where they thought the will had been drafted, the lawyer said that the one he had was null and void because Ernie had gone somewhere else to make a new will just a month before he died.

Maggie took all the wooden puzzles down to the bakery and grew more frustrated that she didn't find the clue as the day went on.

A couple of hours later, the bell over the door rang, and Maggie looked up.

"Hi Maggie, I am so happy to see you!" Judy shrieked as she ran in the door, across the room, and behind the counter to grab Maggie in a big bear hug.

"Hi Judy," Maggie sniffed. "I am so glad you're home."

"Oh honey, let me get you a hankie." Judy handed a beautifully embroidered handkerchief to Maggie and then looked around at the wooden puzzles lying on the counters, which usually held pastries.

"Uh, Maggie, what are you doing?"

"Okay, this will sound crazy, but my dad came to see me last night."

"Oh honey, I need to get you to a doctor." Judy grabbed her hand and started pulling her out from behind the counter.

Maggie planted her feet. "No, Judy, not like that. He came to me in a dream and told me I could find it. We were playing with these wooden puzzles in the dream, as we used to every Saturday morning."

"I remember. Those were some of the best times. While my parents were fighting and breaking dishes, your dad played with us and taught us how to solve problems."

"That's it, Judy. I know the clue is in one of these puzzles. I just have to figure out which one. Unfortunately, I have only gotten through about ten of them, so we have about forty more to solve."

"Well, let's get cracking then."

Maggie was so thankful for Judy, not just because she was helping her solve the puzzles but because she believed her interpretation of the dream. She thought that the clue was in one of the puzzles too.

"Wow, these are harder to solve than I remember."

"I know Judy, it took me longer to figure out than it used to—it has been at least five years since we played with these."

Judy took her cat-eye sunglasses off her head and ran her hands through her hair in frustration.

"Okay, back to work."

They smiled at each other, and Maggie felt better about the future than she had for days.

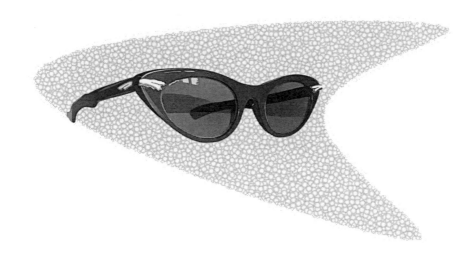

After a couple of hours, they stopped for lunch, and Maggie made some cookies for the display case. Unfortunately, they ran out of almost everything yesterday after her father's funeral, and everyone in the neighborhood came to the bakery. Today's business was slower than most days, but Maggie was relieved to have time to work on the puzzles.

Maggie grabbed a new puzzle and turned the wooden pieces until a sliding compartment was revealed. She slid the piece open and gasped.

"Oh, my goodness, Judy, I found it!"

"Let me see!" Maggie held it out to her, and Judy squinted at it. "What is it?"

"It's a rolled-up piece of paper."

Judy rolled her eyes, "Well, I can see that. So what's on the paper?"

"I think it is a map. There are all these little squiggles on it. And an X to mark the spot."

"Okay, so now we have to figure out the map too?" Judy looked frustrated.

"It shouldn't be too difficult; he'd want us to find it—and he knew that we are the only two who could solve his puzzles."

"Okay, so let's look at the map."

Maggie and Judy sat down at the table to study the map. It had a rectangle with another smaller rectangle inside of it. Maggie looked around the bakery, sure that he'd have placed the next clue somewhere she'd be able to find it. Then it hit her. It looked exactly like the open/close sign that she had turned twice a day her whole life.

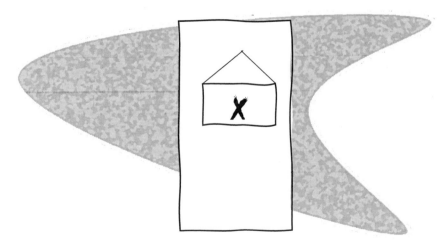

Maggie got up from her chair so quickly that she knocked it to the floor. Then she ran up to the sign and ripped it off the door. As she looked out the window, she thought she saw someone standing across the street smoking a cigarette and watching the bakery.

She was so distracted by the person that she didn't notice Judy coming up behind her.

"What are you looking at?" Judy inquired.

"That guy is just standing on the corner staring at the bakery."

"Maggie! I saw him in the same spot when I came in."

"Well, who do you think he is."

"I don't know. I never saw his face, but I don't like it. We need to solve this problem, and fast."

Maggie locked the door and sat down at the table with Judy. She turned the sign over in her hands, then realized something was stuck inside the sign. There was a frame around the sign; on one side, it said OPEN, and on the other CLOSED. So, there was room between the two signs and a frame around them to keep them in place.

"Judy, there is something wedged inside the frame!" Maggie stuffed her fingers in the frame and came out with a key.

"What do you think the key is for?"

"It looks like a safety deposit box."

Maggie kept digging into the frame and found a piece of paper.

To my most prized treasure, Maggie,

I knew you would find my clue in the puzzle and figure out where I hid the key. I have no doubt that Judy has been helping and supporting you every step of the way. I am glad that you have her.

I am sorry for all the cloak and dagger moves. I received terrible news from my doctor and knew I didn't have long to live. I needed to be sure you were well taken care of.

I need you to know that Bradley has been threatening me and promising he'll put me out of business. Since he works at the bank now, I didn't want to give him the chance to get the bakery, so I had my will redone at another law firm outside the city and put in a safety deposit box for safekeeping.

Maggie, please call the police immediately. Do not trust anyone else. Get them to help you get to the will. I am afraid that Bradley will do something rash. He has never been the most stable man.

Please take care.

I am sorry I had to leave you so soon.

Love you forever

Dad

P.S. I love you too, Judy!

Tears ran down Maggie's face and onto the table.

"Maggie, you need to call the police now."

Just then, someone pounded on the door. "Let me in, Maggie. I know you are in there."

Maggie couldn't see the door from where she was sitting but knew that it was Bradley's voice.

"No, Bradley, I am not letting you in."

"The bakery is mine. It has always been mine."

Maggie motioned for Judy to call the police on the phone in the back room.

"Bradley, it was my dad's bakery, and now he left it to me."

"Once I get in there and destroy the evidence, you will not have a chance to get the bakery."

"Bradley, we have already called the police."

"Good try, Maggie. I have been listening to you girls outside the door since you found the key. But fortunately for me, you never called the police."

Just then, the sound of sirens pierced the air.

Maggie saw Bradley run past the windows away from the wailing sound of the sirens.

"Stop, or we will shoot!"

Maggie saw Bradley pull a gun out of his jacket and point it at the officers.

"Bradley, put the gun down on the ground and put your hands against the wall."

Bradley finally relented and put his gun down. The officers rushed to put him in cuffs. After they put him in the police car, Maggie opened the door for the officers.

"Thank you so much for coming. You were just in time."

"Maggie, your dad told us to watch out for you. He told us all about Bradley. We have been watching him for days."

"He did?"

"He did. Bradley won't be bothering you anymore."

"Officer, I found the key to my dad's safety deposit box, and I am sure the will is there."

How about I take you to get the will now?"

"That would be great." She looked over and Judy and they both said, "Thank you, officer."

Maggie and Judy walked back into the bakery after a long day at the lawyer's office. As expected, Ernie left Maggie everything. Bradley was in jail. And Maggie truly felt that everything would work out okay for her. She'd follow in her father's footsteps, knowing that she was Ernie's treasure.

ABOUT THE AUTHOR

Addison Frost was born in a small town in Minnesota. She studied art history and graphic design and has a master's degree in business. She began writing her debut novel after obsessing over books her whole life. When she's not writing, she can be found wandering through nature or journaling at a coffee shop. Addison currently lives in Minnesota with her husband, daughter and a black cat.

STORY THREE

Future Private Detective

By Lynn Garthwaite

"You're crazy," laughed Tim. "Man landing on the moon? You've been watching too much of that *Star Trek* show."

Mary Jo rolled her eyes as she continued hanging new packs of shower curtain rings in the center aisle of Beck's Hardware Store.

"First of all, shut up, Timbo. They're playing my favorite new Turtles song." She hummed along to the upbeat sounds of "Happy Together" from the speakers embedded in the store's ceiling.

"And wake up, it's nineteen sixty-seven. Anything is possible. NASA's been talking about it ever since John Glenn looped around the earth. Great things are happening. You'll see."

Tim was not convinced. He picked up a box of bolts and walked away, his voice rising as he got to the next aisle. "How would we get that far up in the atmosphere? Where do they refuel? You think there's a Texaco station up there? Maybe man isn't supposed to leave the Earth."

Mary Jo's snippy response was interrupted by the jangle of the door opening at the front of the store. She watched as a man entered, carrying a shoebox full of something to the tube tester near the front windows. The man had a look about him that made Mary Jo uneasy, so she took her place behind the counter, suspecting that perhaps his plan was to steal something.

But instead of stealing, the man set his shoebox down and began to insert his TV tubes into the tester, one at a time. She could tell he was angry about something. Swear words were barely audible under his breath, and he jammed in one tube after another. Her place behind the counter was about twelve feet away, so she called out: "Can I help you with that?"

The man didn't look at her. He continued to shove the TV tubes, one at a time, into the tester until one finally sent the dial to red. He stared at it, then looked around, his eyes searching for the supply of replacement tubes. By that time, Mary Jo had come around the counter and approached him.

"The new ones are in the drawer underneath. What brand is your TV?

"Zenith," he barked as he yanked on the metal drawer built into the testing station and began rifling through stacks of tubes in cardboard sleeves.

"Here, let me help you. The Zenith ones are on the left. Here." She reached in, pulled one out, and handed it to him but froze when she got a look at the tube that was still in the tester in front of her. A tiny smile had been painted on the glass with pink watercolor paint, a detail that would not have caught her attention except that the week before, their own family television had been stolen from their living room. Five years before that, a thirteen-year-old Mary Jo had painted happy smiling faces with her pink watercolor set on a few of the tubes.

She pretended not to notice, but every hair on her arms stood up, and she felt cold. Was this the man who had stolen their tv? Her family had been stuck watching shows on the tiny set in the kitchen until they could afford to replace the larger Zenith set that had taken up part of one wall in the living room.

Careful not to alert the man that she suspected him, she rang up the sale of his new tube and watched him walk to his car, the shoebox under his arm and the small bag with the new tube gripped tightly in his hand.

"Tim!" she called out to her coworker. When he didn't answer, she darted to the break room at the back of the store. "Tim—I have to leave for a couple of minutes. Can you cover for me?"

Tim looked up, confused by the urgency in her voice. "Yeah. I guess. Yeah. Go."

Mary Jo was already racing back to the front of the store before he finished talking. She pushed through the door, setting off the jangling bells, and looked up the street in time to see a red Chrysler Town and Country Wagon stop at the corner a block away. From a distance, she was sure the driver was the man who had just left the store.

With her eyes watching the progress of the station wagon, she yanked her black Schwinn from the bike rack and raced after him. Careful not to get too close to make sure he wouldn't notice her, she followed the car through a series of turns in the residential neighborhood and watched from a distance as he finally turned and parked in a driveway. Still not daring to get closer, she saw the man she recognized from the hardware store walk up the steps and then stop. She held her breath, knowing that if he turned to look, he would almost certainly see her and remember her from the store. But instead of looking around, he pulled on the door handle and went inside, carrying both the shoebox and the bag from the store with him.

So that's where he lives, she thought. It suddenly hit her that she was only three blocks from her own house. He must be stealing from his own neighbors!

Not knowing what to do, she peddled back to the hardware store and finished out her shift. Tim tried to ask what had happened, but she just told him she had to check on something. *Do I call the police? Is there really enough evidence? What if I'm wrong and I send the police to the wrong guy?*

That night, Mary Jo couldn't stop fidgeting at the dinner table. Later, as she and her mom cleared the table, her mom asked if anything was wrong.

"No, I'm fine," Mary Jo lied. "Just tired from work, I guess. But the good news is my bank account keeps growing, and I'm that much closer to having that tuition for a year at junior college! I can't wait to start the classes on criminal justice."

Later that night, when the house was quiet except for the tiny TV in the kitchen, Mary Jo told her parents that she would ride over to her friend Becky's house to watch *The Virginian*.

They waved and didn't suspect her real plans as she rode down the block and rounded the corner.

She rode back to the block where she had followed the man earlier in the day and found a spot far away from the streetlight so she could watch his house without being spotted. Mary Jo wasn't sure what she expected to see, but after about a half hour, she saw the man's front door open and watched as he approached his car in the driveway. When he opened the car door, the light from the dome in the car revealed that he was dressed all in black, which made her buzz with anticipation.

As he drove away, she slowly followed on her bike, again keeping a distance so he wouldn't notice. Finally, after several turns, he slowed down in front of a house that was dark inside. It was early enough in the evening that the residents were unlikely to already be in bed, so Mary Jo suspected he was looking for a house that was empty for the evening.

She watched as he quietly got out of his car, gently closing the door so it wouldn't make a noise, and walked stealthily to the front door. He knocked quietly and stood, listening for someone to come to the door. When no one came, he lifted a small pry bar that he carried in his hand and quickly forced the door open.

Mary Jo couldn't believe what she was seeing. *I have to get to a phone*, she thought. *Should I knock on someone else's door?* While she debated what to do, she saw the man coming

out of the house, carrying what looked to be a large radio and a speaker. He walked quickly to his car, opened the back door, placed the electronics on the back seat, and then got in the front and drove away.

Now Mary Jo was angry. "He can't keep doing that to people. This stops tonight." She picked up her bike and rode in the opposite direction that the man's car had taken to make sure she didn't cross paths with him. She rode to the Brooktown Mall, where many of the stores were still open, and headed directly to the payphone in front of Montgomery Wards.

When the police dispatcher answered the phone, Mary Jo frantically reported that she had just seen a robbery in progress and that she could give them the address of the thief. Thankfully, the dispatcher believed her and took down Mary Jo's name and all of the information relayed to her.

Her hands were shaking when she hung up the phone. She took a couple of deep breaths to calm herself, then got back on her bike and headed home. Two hours later, police officers came to her home and reported that a thief had been caught and that a television matching the one that was in their own police report was in the home of the thief. It would be returned to them soon.

At that point, one of the officers turned to Mary Jo and asked if she was the same Mary Jo Williams who made the call to dispatch. Her parents were shocked when Mary Jo nodded

her head. The officer smiled, shook her hand, and congratulated her on her good work. "You were right not to confront the man yourself. Thank you for calling the station. A lot of people will be getting their stolen goods back, thanks to you."

Mary Jo blushed but was happy for the outcome. And she knew when their own TV was returned, it would have a brand-new tube inside. Perhaps her future career had actually just begun.

ABOUT THE AUTHOR

Lynn Garthwaite is the author of eleven books, including the *Dirkle Smat Adventure* book series, three picture books for clients (Radio Flyer and Shutterfly), and an historic non-fiction for all ages titled *Our States Have Crazy Shapes: Panhandles, Bootheels, Knobs and Points*. She has also written a mystery/thriller: *Starless Midnight* and an updated nursery rhyme book titled *Childhood Rhymes for Modern Times. Your Children Can be Writers: 40 Story Prompts to Spark their Creative Genius* was released in 2022. Lynn is also a copyeditor for three magazines and a publisher, and a member of Sisters in Crime.

GRANDPA'S CAP

By Gloria VanDemmeltraadt

"**O**h, Mom, do I have to?"

"Yes, you do. Your grand-mother is getting older and slower, and her memory isn't what it used to be. You're her only granddaughter, and she expects to see you. You know she misses your grandfather, and life isn't easy for her now. I do what I can, but since he disappeared, she just hasn't been the same. I can't believe it's been six years since he left."

"I can. Grandma used to be fun, but now she's just crabby. I don't know if she misses Grandpa or if she's glad he's gone. I miss him, too. We used to have so much fun, and he always listened to me when nobody else would. Now she doesn't seem to care whether I'm there or not, and she never listens to me."

Grandma lived across town from our family in a house that looked from the outside like it should be pictured in an antique ad from the 1940s. Mom and Dad had done some painting and fixing up of the house. It was the end of the 1960s now, and the kitchen was done in orange. A popular plaid sofa was in the living room with aqua tub chairs. Grandma had insisted on a plastic cover for the sofa because she said Grandpa always spilled on it, even though he wasn't there anymore.

The story about Grandpa was that he just disappeared one day. Grandma said she had sent him to the store for some pickled beets to go with dinner, and he never came home. The store was close by, only a few blocks, and he walked, so the

police didn't have the car to look for when the family reported him missing. In fact, the car was still in the garage, full of gas. The people at the store said he never showed up to get the pickled beets, and they hadn't seen him that day at all. Everyone in our family, plus the police and the neighbors and even strangers, had looked and looked for him, and the police followed up every lead. Mom told me his missing persons case was still open with the police department, and his whereabouts were never determined.

"Please don't be late picking me up, Mom. You know I have homework."

"I know you do, sweetie. Thanks for seeing your Grandma. Give her a kiss for me and tell her I'll be over tomorrow to take her shopping." She took off so fast that the tires squealed.

I rang the bell and walked in. The house took on a lonely, stale smell through the years. It was as though the building itself was missing Grandpa, too, and waiting for him. The distinctive smell hit me in the face like a slap when I opened the door that was always unlocked.

Grandma was sitting in her usual place on the sofa. She had been knitting, but the yarn ball had fallen on the floor and had rolled across the room. She was sleeping with her head bent over the half-finished slipper and the needles stuck out like lethal pointed weapons. Slippers were her current project, and everyone in the family had several pairs of the slippery things already, but they were warm, I will say that.

"Grandma?" I gently poked her arm to let her know I was there. She snorted but didn't wake up. "Well, this is a waste of time," I said to myself. She was totally crashed.

I looked around the house for something to do and almost wished I had brought along my homework. There wasn't much to do at her house other than help with meals or dishes or just try to chat with Grandma. One thing she often told me was to stay out of the attic. Not that I'd want to go in her yukky attic, but now I began to wonder why she didn't want me to go there. The more I thought about it, the more I was curious about what might be up there.

Curiosity won out, but the door was locked. I found an old key in the kitchen junk drawer that might work, and sure enough, it did. Grandma was snoring as I crept up the creaky, dusty stairs, and I closed the door.

There was not much up there except dust, and the light was dim as it tried to pass through the dirt-encrusted window. Old furniture lined the walls, and I found a couple of heavy chests. One was filled with old clothes and was a treasure. Grandma's wedding dress was buried in there, and a fine net slip that went under it. I pulled on the slip and danced around a little, imagining myself to be a doll in a tiny music box. Other precious things included picture albums that I just had to look through. Pictures of my mother looked exactly like me, I was surprised to see, and she was very beautiful. "Maybe there's hope for me yet," I thought.

Pictures of me as a baby, and my brothers, too, were fun to see. I didn't understand why Grandma didn't want me to see the pictures, and there were many of my parents and grandparents together. We had family picnics with lots going on, and I remembered Grandpa reading books to me by the big oak tree in their backyard.

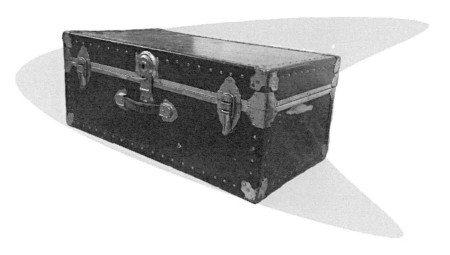

The other chest was locked, and I wondered about that until I saw an iron rod that looked like a fireplace poker by the window. I was well into my hunt by this time, and I was determined to see what other prizes I might find. The poker was covered in rusty red flakes that fell off as I used it to pound the lock, and when it fell apart, I lifted the hefty lid to look inside.

A piece of cloth was under the lid and covered the contents of the chest. The smell was mustier and more rank in this chest, and I closed my eyes, wondering what was under the cloth. The other chest held only my grandmother's clothing and belongings, so I naturally thought that this one might have something that belonged to or was important to Grandpa.

Before peeking under the cloth, I crept down the stairs to check on Grandma. I didn't want her to know that I had deliberately disobeyed her orders to stay out of the attic. She had leaned back in her cozy position on the couch and was still deep in a comfortable nap. I took this as permission and ran back up the stairs and over to the chest.

I quickly pulled off the cloth and opened my eyes, expecting to be surprised, excited, and, hopefully, happy to see what lay beneath.

Instead, what I saw was a ghastly and repulsive human skull wearing my grandpa's favorite cap, and its empty eyes were looking straight at me!

I gasped and scooted backward in shocked surprise. Frozen in a moment of panic, I heard my mother drive into the gravel driveway. I tore down the stairs as she came in the door, ran past still-sleeping Grandma, and whispered, "I found him, Mom. I found Grandpa!"

ABOUT THE AUTHOR

Gloria VanDemmeltraadt
Much of her work focuses on drawing out precious memories. As a hospice volunteer, she continues to hone her gift for capturing life stories and has documented the lives of dozens of patients. She refined this gift in Memories of Lake Elmo, a collection of remembrances telling the evolving story of a charming village. She continues her passion and has caught the essence of her husband's early life in war-torn Indonesia. In Darkness in Paradise, Onno VanDemmeltraadt's story is touchingly told amid the horrors of WWII. This work has been praised by Tom Brokaw and has also earned the New Apple Award for Excellence in Independent Publishing for 2017 as the Solo Medalist for Historical Nonfiction.

The theme of legacy writing continues with a nonfiction booklet, a clear and concise how-to manual called Capturing Your Story: Writing a Memoir Step by Step.

Gloria lives and writes in mid-Minnesota. Contact her through her website: gloriavan.com.

STORY FIVE

Marjorie Penroy's Perfect Day

By Leandra Logan

O n the first Friday of every month, Marjorie Penroy enjoyed a perfect day.

More often than not, the day was a sunny one. If there happened to be a cloud in the sky, Marjorie looked for its silver lining.

This first Friday in June 1964 was seasonally warm and sunny in Saint Paul, Minnesota. Sunlight streamed through Marjorie's bedroom window, as did the warm breeze gently tossing her white dotted-Swiss curtains.

Marjorie didn't need an alarm clock to awaken her. Even on restless nights, she always awoke at six in the morning, just as she had during her childhood days on the farm.

Promptly at six, she sat up in bed, swung her rather shapely legs to the floor, and jammed her feet into her yellow mules. Then she stood, reached for the frilly cotton duster at the foot of her bed, and slipped it on.

Walking to her highboy dresser, she glanced in the mirror and ran arthritic fingers through her soft gray curls. Then, as always, she reached for the photograph of her fiancé, Major Walter Sims, a casualty of World War II.

The man in the black-and-white photograph remained her one and only true love. But while her image in the mirror reflected her advanced age, Walter's frozen image remained vibrant and youthful. He was still the dashing fighter pilot she'd kissed goodbye in February 1942.

Two months later, the Japanese shot down his plane in the Pacific.

She kissed the cool glass layered over the photo and spoke to Walter.

"Miss you, my darling! I will always regret that we waited too long to tie the knot, to have children. But we were busy, you with your military obligations, me with my devotion to my invalid mother. So now, with both you and Mama enjoying your heavenly reward, I find myself often alone.

"But no worries today, Walter. I'm off to enjoy my perfect day. Yes, it's pretty routine each month, and yes, I am on a tight budget in my retirement. But more often, on these special Fridays, I tend to splurge a little bit on myself with a

book or some stationery. After all, with no heirs in sight at sixty-four, there seems no reason to save every single penny anymore."

Marjorie went to the kitchen to eat a light breakfast of eggs, toast, and juice. Then, with a shimmer of excitement, she dressed for her day. First, Marjorie donned her best intimates and topped them off with a pink gingham shirtwaist. Lastly, she exchanged her slippers for comfortable walking shoes, just right for her excursion into downtown Saint Paul.

Before popping out the front door, she thought to check her reflection in the full-length mirror to make sure her slip wasn't showing.

By 9:30, Marjorie had made her way to the corner to catch the bus along Arlington Avenue. Marjorie soon boarded and

dropped her bus fare into a slot near the driver, enjoying the clink the coins made as they fell deep inside the steel tower.

"A very good day to you, Miss Penroy!" Bert, the driver, greeted her with a grin and a nod.

"Good morning, Bert," Marjorie returned brightly.

Bert waited for Marjorie to get comfortable on the extended bench behind him before releasing the brake and urging the bus forward.

The bus rolled down to Rice Street and gradually made its way into downtown Saint Paul. Marjorie smiled at her fellow passengers, the mothers with small squirmy children, the formally dressed professionals likely off to offices and department stores.

Marjorie loved many of the downtown stores: Dayton's, Donaldson's, Grants, and Woolworths. Her first stop today would be Dayton's, as their Daisy Sale was in full swing.

Marjorie descended to the sidewalk at a Dayton's entrance, feeling a gust of hot air scoot up the skirt of her dress. She joined the cluster of ladies in summer frocks with large colorful handbags entering the store.

Daisy Sale signs were posted everywhere, and an air of excitement swirled among the shoppers. Salesgirls strolled the floor, offering tiny sample bottles of high-end perfume or squares of quality chocolates.

Marjorie delighted in both, filling her handbag with the treats to enjoy later.

She lingered in the women's apparel section of the store, trying on a dozen summery dresses. Today's dress was a few years old, and everyone at church would likely remember it from other summers. Finally, she settled on a fashionable sleeveless shift in a floral print. She could accessorize it with a blazer or sweater on cooler days.

Marjorie moved on to the intimate apparel section. She probably didn't need a girdle with her trim hips, but it would smooth out her tummy in more form-fitting clothing. So she decided to buy a new one and a few pairs of stockings.

It was time for lunch, so she headed for Dayton's River Room.

"Good afternoon, Miss Penroy," Flo, the waitress, said, standing by Marjorie's table with her order pad and pencil. "What will it be today?"

"I will have your chef's salad with an extra side of French dressing, two of your trademark popovers, and a cup of coffee."

"Coming right up, Miss Penroy!"

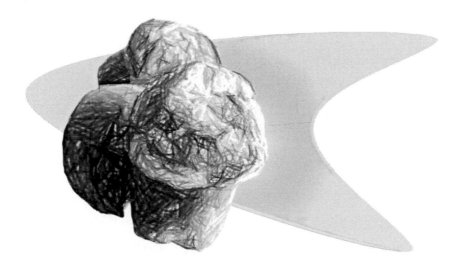

Oh, how Marjorie enjoyed dining in the River Room. She sipped from her stemmed water glass and appreciated the peaceful, sophisticated atmosphere. Ladies and gentlemen dressed to the nines occupied the white linen-covered tables, some conversing over menus and wine lists, some enjoying generous helpings of delicious entrées. The mouthwatering aromas of brewing coffee and oven-baked popovers filled the air.

A few diners recognized Marjorie from her career days downtown and gave her a smile or a nod before returning to their chums. For a brief moment, she envied their shared

companionship. But it was all right. Nothing stayed the same. And women were often overlooked once they turned sixty and allowed their hair to go gray.

After settling her check with a generous tip tacked on, Marjorie collected her paper sacks and headed outside to Woolworths. There, she treated herself to a giant chocolate sundae with whipped cream and sprinkles at the soda fountain, then bought a Duncan yoyo for the neighbor girl who helped Marjorie pull weeds in her garden.

Her last stop of the day was the Midland Bank to deposit her pension check. She entered the bank's lobby, an airy, quiet place of polished gray flooring and pink marble pillars. Grand wooden desks were positioned out front and behind glass walls. Marjorie approached a teller's cage, exchanging waves and smiles as she had with the employees of the River Room. She set her paper sacks on the counter and reached into her handbag for her check and deposit slip.

Suddenly, a scuffle of feet echoed through the hollow room, followed by "Stick 'em up! This is a robbery!"

Frightened cries filled the air as two burly men charged forward, brandishing large guns.

"Listen up, people!" the bigger man yelled. "Go stand against the far wall with my friend. Except for you, lady."

Marjorie cringed when she realized the robber was speaking to her!

"Yeah, I mean you, old timer."

Customers and employees alike scrambled to obey the robber's command. Soon everyone but Marjorie was herded against the wall and held at gunpoint.

The menacing robber jabbed a finger at the Employees Only gate, leading to the cash drawers and safe. "Get behind there." Marjorie grasped her sacks and meekly marched through the wooden gate leading to the cages with his gun inches from her body.

The robber shoved a handled burlap bag at her and pushed her toward the cages. Marjorie teetered and lost her grip on her paper sacks, sending them flying across the polished floor. Her girdle and stockings came spilling out of one for all to see!

"Open the first cash drawer—and make it snappy!"

Marjorie sniffed feebly and clutched the burlap bag to her chest. "Not until you pick up my *unmentionables*," she trailed off in a whisper. "Please. Then I'll kindly do as you say."

With a menacing growl, the robber lumbered several steps and crouched to stuff the underwear back in the Dayton's sack, attempting to keep a sharp eye on Marjorie, who had sagged against the counter.

He stalked over with her sacks and dropped them on the floor at her feet. "Okay. Now start loading up the bills."

Marjorie slowly opened a drawer and squinted at the contents. "Which denominations?"

"Huh?"

"Which bills do you want?"

"Fifties and hundreds. Oh, just gimme all of it!"

Marjorie carefully removed the stacks of bills from their slots and set them gingerly in the burlap bag.

"Get a move on to the next drawer! You're not handling dangerous sticks of dynamite."

Eventually, Marjorie loaded all the bills from all four drawers into the bag and handed it back to the robber. He roughly grasped her arm and hauled her over to the folks standing against the wall.

With orders to stay against the wall for the count of fifty, the robbers charged back out the entrance.

Only the customers started to count. The employees brazenly broke free and scooted close enough to the entrance to gaze outside.

Lo and behold! There was a posse of policemen taking the men into custody.

The bank manager, Russell Jensen, wasted not a moment encircling Marjorie's thin shoulders with his arm. "Nice work, Margie. The moment you deliberately sent your bags skidding and leaned into the counter, I knew you were preparing to step on the silent alarm."

"And you stalled for as long as you could to give the police time to respond," the head teller commended. "Well done."

"What a piece of good luck," the manager said, "that the robbers chose you, a retired bank employee, to do their dirty work."

"It's one of the few instances since my retirement last year when it has felt good to be an invisible old person," Marjorie declared. "It's a sad fact of life that people frequently underestimate older folks. Look right through them."

"I'm sorry if we ever made you feel invisible, Margie," the manager consoled. "We've missed you but figured you were content in your retirement."

By now, the police were streaming in the doors. Russell assured them there were only two robbers.

Marjorie glanced at her watch. "Oh, my! If I don't hurry, I'll miss my bus."

"Not to worry," Russell Jensen said. "No doubt the police will be interviewing you. Afterward, I'll drive you home

myself. Meanwhile, it's time for a Midland Bank cheer. So gather round, everybody!"

The employees assembled around Marjorie and sang out, "Nothing's the matter with Margie! She's all right!"

Safely back at home that evening, Marjorie sat on the edge of her bed with Walter's framed photograph in her hands.

"Oh, Walter, today was the perfect day to end all days! I got samples of perfume and candy at the Daisy Sale. I also bought a fancy new dress and undies there. And believe it or not, I foiled a robbery at Midland. Remember me mentioning my old boss, Mr. Jensen? He has offered me a part-time job at the bank—two days a week, to fill in where needed.

"Am I going to accept? Of course, I am! I hadn't realized how much I missed being around the action until I was back in the thick of things. This past year I was merely fooling myself into believing I was happy on my own.

"Also, I am to receive a three-thousand-dollar reward for helping to capture the crooks. Yes, you heard the amount correctly. It's a small fortune! All summer long, I can buy the neighborhood children treats from the ice cream truck, help my favorite charities, buy a few more dresses, and still have a tidy nest egg for a rainy day."

"I hope you too had a perfect day, Walter." Marjorie pressed her lips against the picture glass. "Goodnight, my love. Goodnight to all."

ABOUT THE AUTHOR

Mary Jane Schultz often writes under the penname Leandra Logan. She is a multi-published, bestselling author in various genres, including romance, mystery, young adult, and illustrated books for children. Mary Jane is a Romantic Times Awards winner and has received numerous nominations within the industry. Her critics praise her for her deeply emotional stories, often lightened with humor, and the red herrings she thoroughly enjoys planting to keep her readers guessing.

Mary Jane resides in the historic town of Stillwater, Minnesota.

STORY SIX
The Neighbor
By Ava Florian Johns

"**C**ome on, Sally, hurry up! The relator is meeting us at the house in ten minutes," James screamed up the stairs.

"Hold on to your shorts. I'll be down in a minute," Salley retorted.

"I swear you'll be late to your own funeral," James said as Sally bounded down the steps two at a time.

"Well, I certainly hope so. Now let's go before we're late."

James rolled his eyes and smiled at his new bride.

Sally and James arrived at the house a few minutes late. The relator was waiting by his car when they got there.

"See, Sally? I told you we'd be late."

"We are not that late. I bet he was early, him and his fancy car."

"That's a beauty. I saw one of those Thunderbirds in the new Ford catalog. I bet he paid a pretty penny for that one. They're going for almost four thousand dollars!"

"What would you do with a fancy car like that? We aren't fancy people. And besides, our car runs just fine. We don't need to worry about new cars. We need to worry about getting a house."

They looked at several homes that were never in their price range. This particular house had been sitting on the market for three years. The realtor said it was because there was a lot

of work to do on the inside. James didn't care. His dad was a construction worker, so he grew up fixing things.

Sally and James got out of the car and turned to look at the house. It was a white one-story rambler with black shutters on the windows and cute planters on the porch. Of course, the planters were empty because no one had lived in the house for so long. It still was more than they had hoped for.

"I love it," Sally whispered to John.

"Don't let on that you want the house; I want to see if I can get him down a few hundred bucks."

"That's why I whispered."

"So, what do you think of the house? Should I get the paperwork started?" the realtor asked.

"Well, we liked to see the inside first."

"Yes, yes, of course, I was getting ahead of myself. As you may have guessed, I'm Ted Carpenter, the realtor." Sally thought he seemed a little nervous, but she knew he had been a realtor for some time, so he shouldn't be anxious about showing a house.

"That's a nice car you have, Mr. Carpenter." Sally jabbed James in the ribs. "Oh, sorry, this is my wife, Sally Evans, and I'm James Evans."

"Mr. Evans, Mrs. Evans, please follow me into your new home."

Sally rolled her eyes at the realtor for being so cocky, but inside she was as excited as a kid on Christmas morning.

The three of them walked together on the sidewalk that led to the concrete step and up to the door. Mr. Carpenter took the key out of his pocket. Sally noticed that his hand was shaking and that he took a deep breath to steady himself before putting the key in the doorknob.

"Are you okay, sir?" Sally asked, more out of curiosity than caring.

"Yes, ma'am, I'm just fine, just a little tired. That sometimes gives me the shakes."

"Do you need any help?" James held out his hand, offering to take the key from Mr. Carpenter.

"Yes, that would be quite nice of you." Mr. Carpenter seemed very relieved not to have to open the door."

James got the door open and let Sally in first, then Mr. Carpenter. James stepped through the door last. As they all entered, they heard loud thumping coming from the back of the house. Mr. Carpenter lost all the color in his face and stood frozen in his spot by the door. He didn't say anything.

"What's that noise?" Sally yelled so she could be heard over the clanging and banging against the side of the house.

"Oh, it's nothing to worry about, Sally. I'm sure that it is just a loose shutter on the back of the house," James declared. Mr. Carpenter still hadn't said a word, and he looked like he was going to faint.

"Mr. Carpenter, can you hear us? What's that noise?" Sally was not sure that James's assessment was accurate. When he

still didn't' answer, James walked over to him and put his hand on his arm. Mr. Carpenter jumped.

"Sorry, I was distracted for a moment. But, yes, you are correct. It is probably just a loose shutter or shingle on the back of the house."

Once he said this, the noise stopped, and they toured the rest of the house without incident. The relator was correct—the house was a fixer-upper. But James seemed excited about doing the work on a home they would call their own.

On the way home, James talked about everything he'd do to make the house their own. Sally couldn't get too excited about the house because she thought something was fishy with it and how the realtor behaved.

Sally wanted to ask James what he thought, but he was busy driving, so she figured she'd wait until they got home.

"What, Sally? You have been thinking about something since we left the house. You haven't said more than two words since we left."

"Aren't you the least bit suspicious about that loud banging sound and the weird way that the realtor was acting?"

"No, not really. He said that it was probably just a loose shutter blowing in the wind knocking against the side of the house."

"He didn't say that you did. He simply agreed with you. And didn't you notice the way he acted when we first got in the house? He didn't want to show us the interior, and he was shaking like a leaf trying to get the key in the doorknob."

"He explained that too. He said he was tired, and sometimes that made him shaky."

"I don't think he was shaky. I think he was scared to walk into the house. What if the house is haunted? Maybe that is why it is so cheap."

"Oh, my dear Sally—you have a very vivid imagination. It is one of the things I love about you."

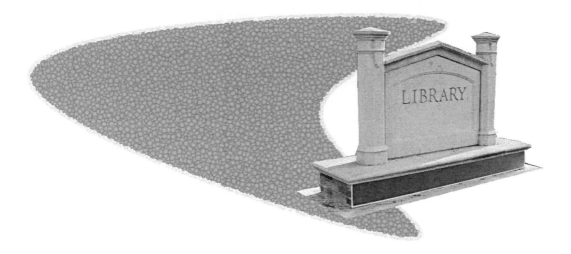

The next day, while James was at work, Sally headed to the library to find information about the house. She hoped that there was nothing wrong with the house because she was sick and tired of living in an apartment building, with people above and below them making noise at all hours of the night. Although she was studying to be a nurse and needed quiet time to read, she didn't get much of it in their apartment.

Sally walked the five blocks to the library and went over to the desk where Miss May worked.

"Hello, Miss May, how are you doing today?"

Miss May was between the ages of sixty and a hundred. No one was quite sure how old she was. All they knew was that she was the best librarian the town ever had, and they were going to let her work as long as she wanted.

"Well, hello there, Sally. I am feeling right as rain. How are you doing today?"

"Good, I came in today because I was hoping you could help me with something."

"Anything, my dear, anything."

"James and I are looking at houses to buy in the neighborhood, and we saw one yesterday that we love. I just wanted to check it out and see if I could find more information about it."

"Can't Mr. Carpenter, the realtor, help you?"

"I don't think he wants to talk about it."

"Well, why ever not? That is his job."

"He seemed nervous about going into the house."

"Oh my. What house are you talking about."

"The white house with the black shutters on Elm Street."

"455 Elm?"

"Yes, how did you know?"

"Because my dear, everyone knows that house is haunted."

Later that day, Sally told James what she'd found out.

"You did what?"

"I went to the library today to research the house and asked Miss May about it."

"And Miss May said it was haunted?"

"Yes, she knew exactly which house I was talking about before giving her the address."

"She is probably trying to drive us away from it so her son can buy it. He is looking for a house too."

"I don't think she'd do that, and I didn't get the impression she was making it up. She sounded like she really believed that the house was haunted."

James thought and asked, "So what do you want to do about it? Should we just give up this house?"

"No, I don't think we should give up. On the contrary, let's investigate."

"Investigate how?"

"I think we should talk to the neighbor. Old Mrs. Henry has lived there for fifty years. If something were going on, she'd know."

"Okay. I guess we can do that. I really want this house, Sally. It would be perfect for us to start a family in."

"I think so too, James, but I want to figure out why people think it is haunted before moving in."

"You don't believe in ghosts, do you, Sally?

"No, but I believe something is going on."

"Okay then, we will talk to old Mrs. Henry tomorrow."

The next day, Sally and James got out of the car at 455 Elm Street and walked around to the back of the house.

"Why are we back here, James? I thought we were going to talk to Mrs. Henry."

"We are, but I thought I'd check out my theory first: a loose shutter or shingle banging against the house."

"I hope you do find something that will explain the noise, but that still wouldn't explain the realtor's behavior."

"No, it wouldn't, but at least we could figure out one thing."

As James looked for something loose, Sally peeked in the house's window and saw an old woman in a long flowing white robe. She looked like a ghost!

"James, come quick. I just saw something."

"What did you see, Sally?"

"Just look in the window."

James walked over to the window and cupped his hands so he could see better.

"I don't see a thing. Other than this window is filthy, all of them will have to be cleaned before moving in."

"James, I saw a ghost. Or what looked like a ghost. It was a really old lady with white hair and a white robe. She looked like she was floating."

"Oh, Sally, all this talk of a haunted house has you seeing things."

"I swear, James, I am not seeing things."

"I think I should get you home so you can rest."

"No, I want to go to the neighbor's house and see what she knows about this ghost."

"Are you sure?" He looked at her and decided not to disagree anymore. If he didn't go with her, he knew she'd go on her own. He recognized the determined look in her eyes.

James grabbed her hand, and they walked across the backyard and around to the front of the neighbor's house. They stood on her step for a moment before knocking on the door. James was worried about Sally and wanted to get to the bottom of it.

James took a deep breath, then knocked on the door.

"Who is it?" They heard the old lady's voice from inside the house.

"It's James and Sally Evans. Mrs. Henry, can we come in for a moment and speak with you about the house next door."

"Um, just a minute."

They could hear some rustling. It sounded like she was moving things around her house to get to the door.

"Yes?" Mrs. Henry said through a small crack in the door. She didn't move to open it any further, so James spoke as close to the gap in the door as he could in case she was hard of hearing.

"Mrs. Henry, can we come in for a minute? We want to speak to you about the house next door."

"What about the house?" she said tersely, still not opening the door.

"Mrs. Henry, I am Sally. I used to see you at the corner grocery store. Do you remember me?"

"No."

"Well, okay. My husband James and I want to buy the house next door to you, but we had a couple of questions."

"It's haunted. Now go away!"

"Mrs. Henry, you don't believe the house is haunted?" James asked in a gentle tone. He didn't want to offend her more than they already had today.

"Yes, I do. Now go away."

"Okay, we are leaving. Thank you for your time," James said.

Sally looked down at the ground, trying to think of a way to get her to open the door. "Oh, Mrs. Henry, here is your newspaper. It was over to the side of the step." Sally reached down to pick it up, so her face was close to the gap in the door

where Mrs. Henry was standing. Mrs. Henry opened the door a bit more to reach her arm out and grab the newspaper from Sally, but Sally noticed something unusual about Mrs. Henry's housecoat. It looked very bulky, making her look much larger than Sally remembered. At the very bottom of the housecoat, there was a strip of white fabric peeking out from the bottom hem.

"Here you go. Thank you for your time." Sally turned to follow James down the driveway.

"Well, that was a waste of time," James complained.

"Not necessarily." Sally smiled.

"What do you mean, and why are you smiling?"

"I mean, it wasn't a waste of time. I figured out who the ghost was. It is Mrs. Henry."

"Why would Mrs. Henry pretend to be a ghost."

"That is the part I don't know, but I bet we could find out."

"How? She won't talk to us."

"But I bet she'd talk to the police."

"Do you want to get the police involved, Sally? She is a little old woman."

"Yes, she is a little old woman hiding something." Sally turned around and headed back up the driveway toward the sidewalk that led to Mrs. Henry's door.

"Where are you going?"

"I am going to try and talk to her again."

"Why?"

"I will get her to tell me why she was in the house next door." Sally got that determined look in her eyes again. The look that James knew better than to argue with.

This time Sally knocked on the front door.

"Mrs. Henry, please open the door. It is us again."

"What do you want?"

"I want you to tell us the truth."

"I'm going to call the police."

"Please go ahead. I'd love to hear you explain to the police why you were pretending to be a ghost to scare potential buyers away from the house next door."

Silence came from the other side of the door. Sally and James couldn't hear anything but the chirping of the birds in the yard. James was about to say they should go when the front door opened, and Mrs. Henry stood before them in her bulky robes.

"Come in."

They stumbled over themselves to get in the house before she shut the door.

"Have a seat, and I will explain it to you. I have been holding the secret in my heart for so long it is time to tell you what I have been hiding."

"Okay, Mrs. Henry, we are listening," Sally said as she reached out and took her hand.

"Thank you, dear. You were the nicest worker at the grocery store. You always carried my bags for me." She cleared

her throat and stared straight ahead, not looking at either. "Three years ago, the week after my husband died, my grandson, Ted, came over and helped me clean the attic. He brought down a big trunk of my husband Ira's. That night, I went through the trunk and found items from the past. The movie tickets from our first date, the photo of us from the carnival, and other things from our life together. I thought what a treasure I have found." Mrs. Henry stopped talking and started softly weeping.

"You don't have to continue if it is too hard for you," Sally said as she handed her handkerchief to Mrs. Henry.

"No, it's time to get this out in the open. My Ira was a good man, but he had a wandering eye. All the things in the trunk reminded me of happier times. As the years went on, I found out that he was having affairs. Then about twenty years ago, I discovered he was having an affair with my best friend. Our next door neighbor, Betty."

"Oh my gosh, that must have been terrible for you." Sally's eyes were overflowing with tears. James reached for her hand and held it.

"It was harder to accept the deception from my friend Betty than my husband, Ira. She listened to me go on and on about Ira's cheating ways, and she never said a word. So the day I found out, I confronted her. She apologized and said that she was in love with Ira and wasn't giving him up." Mrs. Henry paused for a moment and looked up at James and Sally.

"I didn't mean for it to happen."

"What happened?" Sally and James said at the same time.

"I threw a vase at her and walked out the door. She was still screaming at me when I left."

"What happened then?"

"I went back to my house and waited for Ira to come home. When he did, I told him what had happened. He told me he'd go next door and end it with Betty once and for all."

"So did he?"

"Well, he was gone for a really long time. I waited by the door. I heard him digging around in the garage, and the tool shed, but I didn't' think anything of it. Then, finally, he came back in and said that he had helped Betty pack her things and walked her to the bus station. She had left for good."

"So everything worked out fine?" Sally was hesitant to ask. She figured the story wasn't over yet.

"That's what I thought. But when I searched the trunk three years ago, I came upon several journals that Ira was keeping. He wrote in it every day that we were married, and I never asked to see what he was writing. Finally, I found the journal he wrote in when he was seeing Betty. He felt terrible for deceiving me, and he was going to break up with her. But then I went over to see her." She took a deep breath before she continued and looked at them as she finished the story. "When he went over to end it with Betty, she was lying dead on the

floor." Sally and James gasped as Mrs. Henry continued her story. "I killed her."

No one said anything for a few moments. Sally and James looked at each other—stunned. "But that still doesn't explain why you keep people away from the house," James said.

"No, it doesn't. See, Ira didn't want me to get in trouble for killing Betty, so he took her body and put her inside the wall. She had been doing some remodeling, and there was an exposed wall. So he put her body inside and built the wall, burying her inside her own house."

"But how is it that no one reported her missing or came looking for her?"

"She didn't have any family, and the only friends she had were Ira and me."

"So other people lived there for seventeen years. With Betty in the wall?"

"Yes, but when I found the journal, I couldn't bear for anyone else to live there, and I couldn't move her, so I made up the ghost story. I'd take a frying pan and bang it on the pipes on the side of the house. Then, when someone comes out, I go into my yard, or I come out and ask them what the noise was. They never suspected me for a minute."

James resisted the urge to laugh.

"So what now?" Sally asked Mrs. Henry.

"Now we call the cops and we give Betty a real burial—one outside the wall—it's time" Mrs. Henry sighed. "It's time.

Two months later, Sally and James moved into their new house, a different one than Betty was in.

ABOUT THE AUTHOR

Ava Florian Johns writes in the science fiction genre. Her characters are clever and fearless, but in real life, Ava is afraid of her basement, bees, and especially clowns. Truth be told Ava wouldn't last five minutes in one of her books.

Ava is best known for her *Omega Team Series*.

STORY SEVEN

THE REUNION CLASS
OF 1949

By Addison Frost

It was the summer of 1969, and it was the twentieth reunion of the Evans High School graduating class of 1949.

"What do you mean you're not going?" Peggy screamed into the phone. "This reunion is all you talked about for months. You lost thirty pounds, dyed your hair, bought a new outfit, and now you are not going?" Mary flinched at Peggy's outburst, suddenly feeling like a child.

Although Peggy and Mary knew each other in high school, they were never friends. Then, two months ago, Peggy contacted her, and they'd been hanging out ever since. But Mary wondered why. Clearly, Peggy didn't like her very much.

"I just thought I'd stay home with you since you can't come," Mary said sheepishly.

"Oh, that sounds just great," Peggy said sarcastically. "You are going to the reunion, end of discussion." Peggy hung up the phone.

"Goodbye to you too."

Mary knew something was fishy when Peggy had first called her. She couldn't understand why Peggy wanted to hang out with her. They hadn't been in the same friend group in school: Peggy was popular and Mary was not, so they had nothing in common. When they were together, Peggy mainly criticized her, or she quizzed Mary about her old boyfriend, who sadly died while they were seniors in high school. Mary couldn't understand why Peggy was interested in being her friend.

Oh well, good riddance. She wouldn't be hanging around Peggy anymore, and frankly, she was relieved to be going on her own tonight. Mary had several other friends that were going to be at the reunion, so she'd hang out with them—they were a lot more pleasant.

Mary finished getting ready and put on her green shift dress that matched the color of her eyes and looked great with her new side-swept bob haircut. A favorite of the decade, shift dresses were a signature '60s style. And, with the extra bit of weight she lost, the shift dress fit her like a glove.

Mary locked up her apartment and headed to the reunion—alone. She was happy to meet her friends at the town's event center but felt a stab of envy. At thirty-eight years old, she was

the only single one in the group; all her friends were married with kids. That was the only reason she had been hanging out with Peggy for the last couple of months—she was one of the only single ones left too.

It wasn't as if she hadn't been proposed to. She had. Five times to be exact, but no one could compare to the first boy that ever asked her—Danny. He was her one true love, and he died in a tragic accent when he was only eighteen years old. She dated some nice men after Danny, but none of them felt like the love of her life. *Maybe you only get one,* Mary thought.

The event center was transformed by white twinkly lights and miles and miles of crepe paper. She checked in at the main table and walked into the ballroom. There, her classmates were dancing to the hits of 1949. Right now, the band was playing "Some Enchanted Evening."

The reunion committee sent out a letter asking for a list of their favorite songs from high school. Mary gave them a few, but she wasn't as into music as the rest of her friends.

"Hey Mary, over here!" Suzie waved her hands in the air to get Mary's attention. As Mary moved toward Suzie, she glanced in the direction of Peggy's friend's table. All the popular girls of their class were there—the reunion planners—and they were all staring at her. She felt like it took forever to reach Suzie.

"Hey Suz, how are you doing?"

"Groovy. I am so glad that you decided to come. The music is far out." Suzie wrapped her arm around Mary and steered her toward the table. "And I am so glad that Peggy got sick and couldn't make it."

"That's not very nice." Then Mary laughed, "But I have to say I am relieved that she couldn't come tonight."

"I will never understand why you have been hanging out with her for the last couple of months."

"I don't know. I have been feeling like the third wheel lately. All of you are married and have kids, and I felt lonely."

"Oh, Mary, that doesn't mean you need to hang out with nasty Peggy. We have all been married for a while now, and you know you are always welcome to hang out with us."

"I know. I just think that I should have accepted one of the proposals."

"No, those men weren't right for you. Someone will come along that will sweep you off your feet. I know, let's get the group together and go on a girls-only trip to Chicago! We could kick up our heels and have a great time. What do you say, Mary?"

"I think that sounds great." Mary turned to see Donald, the football team captain, class president, and class cum laude, take the stage.

Mary thought, *He is still gorgeous—it is hard to believe he's still single.*

"Hello, class of 1949, and welcome to our twenty-year class reunion." He paused until the applause died down. "I am Donald Carlson." Chants from the football team of "Donny, Donny, Donny" filled the room. "Settle down. I want you to know that the reunion committee has a huge surprise for all of you. After dinner and a little more drinking, the committee will hand out the time capsules that we buried in the schoolyard before we graduated. The school broke ground on a new building and found them and thought it would be a great surprise for us. So, enjoy your meal and some dancing, and we will be back to you soon."

"Wow, Donald is still gorgeous, and I heard he's still single." Suzie mirrored Mary's thoughts.

"I know. I wonder why. I heard that he is very successful, nice, and still extremely handsome," Mary said wistfully.

"I don't know, but there must be something wrong with him."

"Oh, Suzie, that wasn't very nice." They both started laughing.

"Oh, Mary, we all know I was never the nice one you were. Don't look now, but Donald is on his way over here."

"What for?"

"I don't know, but I bet he is not coming over to talk to me."

"Hey Suzie, Mary, how are you doing?" He put more emphasis on Mary's name. Mary just stood silently until Suzie answered.

"We're doing great, Donald. Right, Mary?"

"Ya, we're doing great." Mary could feel Donald's eyes on her.

"That is great news about us getting to see our time capsules. But unfortunately, I can't remember what I put in mine," Suzie said, imploring Mary with her eyes to contribute to the conversation.

"Me either, but I bet the items were all significant to my eighteen-year-old self." Mary looked sad, remembering the days surrounding graduation.

"I remember that wasn't a great time for you. You just lost your—Danny." Donald stuttered a bit.

"Yes, a week before I made the time capsule."

"I'm so sorry, Mary. He was a great guy."

"Yes, he was." Mary was taken aback at how friendly Donald was, but he had always been a nice guy. Even though he was super popular, he always had time for her.

"Donald, isn't it time you came over and talked to us," Sherry purred from the cool table.

"Just a minute, Sherry." He turned to Mary and whispered, "Save me a dance, sweet Mary."

Once he was out of hearing range, Suzie screamed, "What did he say to you?"

"He asked me to save him a dance."

"Oh my. That is fantastic," Suzie gushed.

"Let's just get to our table. I am sure our food is getting cold."

They finished eating, and the music started up again. Sure enough, Donald came over to the table to ask Mary for a dance.

"Can I have this dance?"

"Yes, Donald, I'd like that very much."

The song the band was playing was "I'll Never Fall in Love Again," by Tom Jones. *How appropriate*, Mary thought.

Donald and Mary held each other as they danced. It was the first time Mary had felt anything for a man in years.

"Mary, I have a confession to make. I really liked you in high school."

"You did? Why?"

Donald laughed. "Because you were so different from the other girls." He made a motion toward the popular girl's table. "That's a good thing."

One of Peggy's friends got up on stage and grabbed the microphone from the singer. The singer gave her a dirty look.

"Hello everyone. I'm Sally, the head of the reunion committee. It's *time* to reveal the time capsules." She laughed at her own joke.

Everyone, including Danny and Mary, stood on the dance floor.

"Go back to your seats!" Sally barked. "We will be bringing your capsules around to your tables. The school has held on to them for the last couple of months and brought them directly here. Fortunately, we sealed them up pretty well, so you will

need to use a knife or scissors to get the capsules open. Alright, everyone, have fun."

Mary and Danny started to walk to their separate tables.

"Mary, can we finish our dance later?"

"Okay people, move it. Get to your tables," Sally yelled into the microphone.

Mary started laughing. "I guess I better get to my table. But, Donald, yes, I'd love to dance with you again."

Mary sat down next to Suzie and the others.

"Wow, you are positively glowing."

"Thanks, he is a very nice man."

"I don't think you are glowing because he is a just nice man. You're attracted to him."

They set down Mary's time capsule with tools for the whole table in front of her. But Mary knew that the contents of this capsule wouldn't be happy memories for her. At that time of her life, she had just seen the love of her life die in an accident, and she was not in the right frame of mind to be participating in the graduation festivities, but her parents made her go to school and finish out the year.

"Okay, Mary, are you ready to crack them open?"

Mary just nodded and started to work on getting the tape off the time capsule. Unfortunately, just as she began tearing the tape off, the lights in the ballroom went out.

THUMP!

"What happened?" Suzie cried. "Mary, are you okay?"

The lights flickered on, and Suzie discovered Mary was lying on the floor. "Yes, I'm okay."

"What happened?"

"Someone knocked me over in my chair and grabbed my time capsule." Mary stood, rubbing her head where it had hit the floor.

"Why?"

"I have no idea." She looked around the room and noticed Donald staring at her. "I bet it was him."

"Donald? Why would you think Donald would come over here, steal your time capsule and knock you on the floor?"

"I don't know, but it makes sense that he was so nice to me tonight and danced with me. Why else would he want to do that?"

"Because he likes you. I think he has always liked you."

"Mary, are you okay?" Donald was suddenly standing next to her. Mary noticed that the music had stopped, and everyone was staring at them.

"Yes, I'm fine, but someone stole my time capsule."

"Who would steal it?" Donald was perplexed.

"Someone who thought something valuable was in it," Suzie chimed in.

"Who would that be?" Donald asked.

"I am guessing it was one of Peggy's friends, probably Sally." Mary pointed to their table, and the people in the room gasped.

"Why would you say that?" Donald inquired.

"Because Peggy befriended me about two months ago. I couldn't figure out why, but I did tonight when we talked about Danny. I told her that I put the engagement ring Danny gave me into my time capsule."

"You did? You never told me that, Mary." Suzie looked hurt.

"I didn't tell anyone. Peggy asked me so many questions about Danny I figured that was what she was after—something that had to do with him. But I didn't figure it out until Donald announced that they found our time capsules. Then, after we graduated, people said they saw me put my ring in the capsule. They joked that they were going to dig it up. I bet that Peggy thought they could steal the ring from the capsule and no one would figure it out. But there was one thing I didn't tell Peggy."

"What was that?"

"I never put the ring in the time capsule. Instead, I gave a ring to Danny's father. I figured out that it was his mother's, and I couldn't in good conscious bury it when Danny's family could have it back.

"So all of this was because of a ring?" Donald was still a little confused. "I just can't believe that Peggy and her friends would go through this much work for a ring."

"Hey, don't blame us. It was all Peggy's idea," Sally wailed from across the room. "The only thing I did was cut the lights."

"So, who grabbed the time capsule?" Mary asked Peggy's friends. They all shrugged their shoulders and looked like they would rather be anywhere but at the reunion.

Before they could answer, Peggy came through the door screaming. "I can't believe I wasted the last two months being your friend."

"That's exactly what I was going to say." Mary smiled.

"Why you little—" Peggy ran up to Mary screaming.

Donald stepped between them right as Peggy was about to grab Mary. "That's enough, Peggy."

"Don't you tell me it's enough? Mary led me to believe that the ring was in the time capsule."

"And you committed petty theft and assault, intentionally putting another person in reasonable harmful or offensive contact."

"How do you know?"

"Because I am a lawyer telling you that you could be charged with two crimes tonight."

"No, I just wanted the ring buried in the ground." Peggy sobbed, placing her head in her hands.

"But it wasn't your ring." Mary had been silent the whole time Donald talked to Peggy but felt that she should add her two cents.

"But I loved him," Peggy wailed. "I loved him more than anything."

"Who?" Donald asked.

"She loved Danny. That's why she wanted it." So Mary finally figured out why Peggy wanted to be her friend, and she finally figured out Peggy a little bit better.

"Well, it's up to you, Mary. Do you want to press charges?"

Peggy looked up at Mary with her tear-stained face.

"No, I think we have all lost enough."

Peggy ran over and hugged Mary, and all of Peggy's friends came to console her.

When the dust settled, Donald and Mary finally finished their dance.

ABOUT THE AUTHOR

Addison Frost was born in a small town in Minnesota. She studied art history and graphic design and has a master's degree in business. She began writing her debut novel after obsessing over books her whole life. When she's not writing, she can be found wandering through nature or journaling at a coffee shop. Addison currently lives in Minnesota with her husband, daughter and a black cat.

Class Reunion

1949

STORY EIGHT
SUSPICIOUS FIRE
By Gloria VanDemmeltraadt

The year is 1956. I am Linda Anderson, a sophomore in high school in a small town that also hosts a prestigious private college. My family's financial status pretty much dictates that I will not be a scholar at the ivy-league school, but I come into daily contact with students of every kind.

My dad owns a small but popular ice cream shop on Main Street. Our family has owned the shop for several years, and I have worked there after school since I could lean far enough into the ice cream counter to reach the goods to make a cone. On not-so-busy days, I also mop the black-and-white checkered floor and clean the red-topped stools, among other jobs.

The shop sells new drinks like Cherry Cokes from our soda fountain, plus the old standbys of Nesbitt's Orange and 7-Up. Dad's Root Beer floats are great, and sundaes, malts, and cones are always popular. My personal favorite is a strawberry sundae, and I always eat the cherry on top of the whipped cream first.

High school and college boys usually work the soda fountain; jerks, they call them, and from my viewpoint, that's an appropriate name. I'm not what you would call a beauty with my mousy brown hair and glasses, and the soda jerks, always on the lookout for a pretty face, regularly let me know I don't fit in that category. However, I am observant, quiet, and thoughtful, and not much happens in the shop, the school, and the town that I don't know about.

For example, something odd happened the other day. We have a payphone in the back of the shop. Dad is still complaining about it going up from a nickel to a dime, but it's still well-used. Kids call for rides home or are looking for others to share a good time and such. A couple of guys were hogging the phone for longer than necessary. They weren't the typical college student types—clean-cut and wealthy-looking nerds; they were older-looking and sort of shifty and sly. I didn't trust them on sight and kept watch of them. Then, just as I was going to call my dad's attention to them, they left.

Today, we had windows open at school on this beautiful early spring day when we abruptly heard screaming fire trucks and even an ambulance rushing by. Mr. Overland kept yelling at us to sit down, but the entire roomful of bored-with-geometry students ran to the windows to see what was going on. Then, finally, my friend Jane said, "Wow, something really bad must have happened! I wonder what it was?"

Of course, we all wondered, and geometry was at the bottom of the list of topics of discussion for the afternoon.

By the time I get to the shop today, it's packed to bursting with townspeople gossiping and sharing what little they know about the sirens. After running myself ragged delivering burgers and fries and malts up to the closing time at nine, no one seems to have any details.

Jane is waiting for me at the shop's back door as we had previously arranged, and we're determined to find out what happened that led to the sirens. Jumping on our bikes, we follow the smell of smoke through town and find one remaining fire truck with two worn-out firemen at the old house near the library. Hazel Cuthbert lives there, and my breath catches as we look over the smoldering hulk of what had been her huge and beautiful old house.

White-haired and ancient, Hazel and I are strange friends because we both love books more than anything. As I was growing up, we'd often find ourselves checking out the same books from the town library, our favorite place, and attending the same speeches and lectures. She finally approached me one day, saying, "I know you're the young Anderson girl from the ice cream shop. It looks like you love books almost as much as I do."

"Yes, that's me." I was a little scared of her because we all knew she lived alone in her mansion, and some people called her a witch, but nobody really knew much about her. She followed up with, "What's the best book you've ever read?" I didn't even have to think and answered, *"The Secret Garden."*

She grinned while saying back to me, "I knew you were someone special. That's my favorite book, too!" After that, she and I began to talk about books whenever we had the chance. She even invited me into her house, where she has her very own library with almost as many books as the town library. That's where I learned to drink tea with lots of milk and sugar. Whenever I can get away from the shop after school or on Saturdays, she and I have what she calls "tea and conversation."

Jane and I lean on our bikes and look over the mess left of my friend's home, particularly the smoking ruins of hundreds of precious books.

Tears are falling, and knowing Jane as well as I do, I don't even care. She hands me a tissue and says, "I know you really like Miss Cuthbert. I hope she's okay."

"Hearing that ambulance scared me today. Now I know why. I'm going to do whatever I can to help her find out what happened here. Are you with me?"

"You betcha!" Jane answers, and we pedal off to our homes.

The next morning is Saturday, but I am up early and glued to the radio in the kitchen, listening to the news about the fire. Sadly, I learn that Hazel Cuthbert has died in the fire. Even worse, I hear that the police say the fire is suspicious. What a terrible word. *Suspicious.*

I call Jane to tell her the terrible news. We agree the suspicious fire is something we need to find out more about, and we bike over to look at the house again. Standing near the pile of rubble, I feel like my heart has been stabbed. Others mill around the site, curious onlookers mumbling among themselves. I look at them, wondering what their connection to my friend might have been.

Suddenly, I see the two sly-looking men who were in the shop the other day. They are sort of sneaking around the ruins and poking at half-burned furniture with a stick. I nudge Jane, "What are they doing here?" She hasn't noticed anything and responds with "Huh?"

I pull her behind a tree, "I don't trust those guys one bit, and we're going to follow them." Always willing for an adventure, she says, "I'm with you," and we crouch down and watch them as they get into an older car. It's a good thing the town is small because speeds are slow, and it's easy for us to follow on our bikes.

They go to an older motel at the edge of town near the railroad tracks, and we see them enter one of a string of paint-chipped doors. It's number seven. Jane and I pull our bikes behind some trees and wonder what to do now. Finally, Jane says, "You know, my uncle Tim is a policeman. Maybe you should talk to him about these guys. This whole thing is scaring me, and I have a stupid dentist appointment that my mom made, so I have to go soon. What do you think?"

"I think I'm going to find out what happened to my friend. I'm just mad enough right now to call your uncle Tim. So, you take off, and I'll go to the shop to call him. I'll let you know what he says." I gulp in false bravery as we pedal off.

I get to the shop a little winded, and my dad says, "Well, here comes Princess Linda. Did you have a good beauty sleep while the dishes piled up waiting for you?"

Ugh. I forgot that I had agreed to help in the kitchen today. "Yeah, Dad, I'll get on it, but first, I have to make a phone call. I've got a dime."

My dad put his arm around me, "Wait a minute, sweetie, are you okay? You look a little flushed, and being late isn't like you. Wanna talk?"

Grateful for his kindness, I say, "I have to talk to somebody, Dad. My friend has been killed. Her house burned down, and I think I know who did it!"

"Whoa here, is this about that old lady who lived by the library? I know you spent time with her and liked her, but this is serious."

"Yes, it's serious, and I need to talk with the police. Do you believe me?"

"Of course I believe you, but how about we have them come here, and I'll be with you while you explain whatever it is that you know? Does that work?" Much relieved, I nod.

Dad then calls the police, and they say an officer will be coming by shortly. I make myself a strawberry sundae while waiting and decide the dishes can wait.

I've never appreciated my dad as much as this moment. He sits close to me as I tell what I know and suspect about the two men. Uncle Tim, or Officer Brady, is a big man; actually, his dark uniform is bulging and dripping with handcuffs, holsters, and frightening paraphernalia all over it. I tell him the whole thing just doesn't feel right with those two, and I am grateful beyond measure that the officer really listens to my feelings. I am also glad that he shares information about Hazel and the fire they know was started by a lantern.

Later, as I scrub the dishes and clean the whole kitchen, I feel immensely relieved and know I did the right thing.

Late that afternoon, as I finish my homework, the doorbell rings. Mom answers it, and sure enough, it is Officer Brady. He asks for me, and I hurtle down the steps.

Mom stays with me as he tells me what transpired after hearing what I had to say. He and another officer went to the motel immediately after he and I talked. He said as soon as the men saw the police, they started making excuses, and it took only minutes before they both confessed to the crime.

It seems that one of the two creepy men is a distant nephew of Hazel, and he heard family gossip that she had a lot of money squirreled away in her house. So, he and his friend decided to break into her house and rob her on a whim. They

thought she wasn't home, but she surprised them as she came down the stairs carrying an old-fashioned lantern. They knocked her down the steps, and the lantern went flying. It landed on some fabric she had lying on a chair and started everything on fire. The men frantically searched for money as long as they dared and then ran off before getting burned. Unconscious Hazel, however, was left to her fate and died in the fire. A terrible tragedy.

Office Brady comes to the shop to see me a couple of days later. He says I am to get some sort of award or medal or something for contacting the police because it led them to them apprehending the perpetrators. It also comes out that Hazel kept her money in the bank, and upon her death, every penny went to the town library.

After this exciting adventure, Jane and I are talking about becoming female detectives when we graduate. I can hardly wait!

ABOUT THE AUTHOR

Gloria VanDemmeltraadt

Much of her work focuses on drawing out precious memories. As a hospice volunteer, she continues to hone her gift for capturing life   stories and has documented the lives of dozens of patients. She refined this gift in Memories of Lake Elmo, a collection of remembrances telling the evolving story of a charming village. She continues her passion and has caught the essence of her husband's early life in war-torn Indonesia. In Darkness in Paradise, Onno VanDemmeltraadt's story is touchingly told amid the horrors of WWII. This work has been praised by Tom Brokaw and has also earned the New Apple Award for Excellence in Independent Publishing for 2017 as the Solo Medalist for Historical Nonfiction.

The theme of legacy writing continues with a nonfiction booklet, a clear and concise how-to manual called Capturing Your Story: Writing a Memoir Step by Step. Gloria lives and writes in mid-Minnesota. Contact her through her website: gloriavan.com.

WHAT'LL YOU HAVE?
By Ann Aubitz

Chucky's Diner was the place teenagers went to eat burgers, listen to the jukebox, and show off their hot rods. Bright and glowing inside and out, Chucky's Diner was bold and energetic.

"What'll you have, boys?"

"Ahh..."

"Come on. I haven't got all day."

"Cool your jets, Mary. Let the boys have a minute to decide."

"I have given them more than a minute. If they are not going to eat, they can't stay. You know the rules, Eddy."

"I'll be right back, boys, and you better order something when I return."

Mary turned and roller-skated toward the kitchen with Eddy, the cook at the diner. She could hear the teenage boys sliding out of the red leather booth and running to the door like their tails were on fire.

"No need to flip your lid, Mary. The boys just want to listen to music and watch the pretty girls come in."

"Well, they don't have to do it during my shift. They are taking up a table."

"What has got your undies in a bunch?"

"Keep talking, Eddy, and you will get a knuckle sandwich."

"Are you really going to hit me? What is going on with you? You've been crabby all week, now spill."

Eddy stopped and turned to look at Mary. She wasn't saying anything. They just stared at each other for a moment. Then Mary realized the moment stretched just a little too long for comfort.

"Why don't you *take a picture,* Eddy? It'll last longer."

"I just wanted to know why you have been so crabby lately, that's all."

"Mind your own beeswax."

"Oh, come on, Mary, I just want to help. We've been working together for ten years. We've been friends our whole lives, now tell me what's wrong?"

"Fine, I have been getting notes all week from someone." Mary paused.

"Well, who are they from?"

"That's the problem. I don't know."

"That's what has you so upset?"

Eddy stepped toward her and was going to hug her, but she rolled backward to get out of his range.

"Yes, that is what has me so upset."

"Why? Are they bad notes?"

"No, it is just confusing. They seem to be from a secret admirer, but why not just come out and tell me?"

"Maybe it's from someone who is too shy to tell you how he feels?"

"Or maybe it's those teenage boys messing with me." She threw her hands up in frustration.

"Is that all that is bothering you? It seems bigger than that."

Mary was about to answer Eddy's question when a customer bellowing from the other room interrupted them.

"Waitress! Can I get some service?"

"Gotta go, Eddy."

Mary skated to the front of the diner to help the customer who sat at the same booth that the boys had just vacated.

"What'll you have?"

"I'd like the meatloaf with mashed potatoes and gravy. Also, a chocolate milkshake."

"Will that be all?"

"Could you step on it? I am in a hurry." The customer seemed really agitated and kept watching the door.

"Yes, sir."

Mary rolled her eyes as she turned and skated on the black-and-white tiles back to the kitchen.

"Order up." Eddy put the food in the window.

"I see it."

"Geez, Mary, you need to be a little nicer. Maybe the guy leaving the notes is just trying to brighten your day."

Mary didn't say anything. Instead, she picked up the tray of food and rolled over to the table of four teenagers waiting for their hamburgers and fries. She set the food in front of them without so much as a "thank you" from them.

"You're welcome." She said in a sarcastic tone as she rolled away.

"Miss, could you please bring me some water," yelled the man who was in a hurry.

"Coming right up," Mary said automatically.

"Ug, the service here is terrible." The guy at the table said.

"What was that?"

"Mary, don't do it. It's not worth it." Eddy stepped out of the kitchen with his spatula in his hand.

"Sir, I will get you your water right now."

Eddy was sure that she'd pour it all over the guy's head, but she didn't. Instead, she set it down in front of him with a sweet smile.

Knowing he wouldn't say thank you, she said, "You are very welcome."

"Just bring me my food and leave me alone" He didn't look up at Mary; instead, he stared at the door.

"Got it."

She looked down at the customer and realized he was fidgeting with something in his hands, but she couldn't see it. Maybe she was making him more agitated than he already was.

Mary rolled over to where Eddy was standing, just outside the kitchen.

"Well, that went better than I expected."

"I will not lose my job over someone like him, and I think he is just having a bad day. You know that Chucky would fire me for throwing water on a customer."

"Yes, even though he loves you, he probably would," Eddy said as he hurried back to the kitchen to dish up the order of meatloaf, mashed potatoes, and gravy.

"Since he is my uncle, I love him too. But I don't know what I will do when he sells the place."

"Do you know if he has any interest?"

"I don't think so. He doesn't really talk about it. I'm worried he'll sell it to a jerk that wants to change everything. I love it just the way it is."

"Order up."

"Eddy, I see the order is ready. I'm standing right in front of you."

"Just making sure, you know, because your customer is in a hurry."

"I am so glad it's almost closing time. You are really getting on my nerves."

She delivered the man's meatloaf and reminded him the diner would be closing in twenty minutes.

Mary couldn't wait for her shift to end. She loved working at the diner, but lately, she felt that her life wasn't going anywhere. She was twenty-six years old, and by this point, she thought she'd be married with kids. But that isn't the way things worked out.

She and Eddy got jobs at the diner the summer they both turned sixteen. Since they were in diapers, they had done everything together—they were best friends. Their parents had gone to high school together, and they all lived in the same small town.

Part of her restlessness was that she didn't know what she wanted. She knew that she loved the diner, but she always

thought that her uncle Chucky would leave it to her. Now that he was selling, that didn't seem to be the case.

She was worried the new boss would be horrible and change everything she loved about the diner. Well, she just couldn't let that happen.

As she pulled her skates off, there was a rap at the glass door. Mary yelled, "We're closed. Come back tomorrow."

"Mary, it's the police. Open up."

"What do you want, Frank? I am all out of donuts."

"Very funny, Mary, open the door."

"I'm coming, bossy pants."

"That's sergeant bossy pants to you."

"How are you tonight, oh brother of mine? Do you want a cup of coffee?"

"No, I am here on official business."

"Official business, what it is?"

"Where's Eddy?"

"He's in the cooler cleaning up." Mary pointed to the back like Frank didn't know where the cooler was. Her had brother worked there for more years than she had. That is until he graduated from the police academy.

"Hey Eddy, can you come out here a minute?" Frank yelled across the diner.

"Geez, Frank, all you had to do was ask me to go get him."

"What's all the yelling about? Frank, what you are you doing here."

"I need to talk to you and Mary about one of the customers that could have come here tonight. Do you recognize this man?" Frank pulled out a photo of a man and showed it to Mary and Eddy.

"Sure do. That's the man that Mary almost dumped water on tonight."

"She what?" Frank looked horrified.

"Oh, don't be so dramatic, you two. I was very nice to him after he snapped at me and told me we had lousy service."

"Where was he sitting?"

"Right there in that booth, why?" Eddy asked, looking confused. "Why are you asking us so many questions about this rude customer?"

"Because we think he robbed the jewelry store in the Landsberg about thirty miles north of here. Their police officers followed him to Sunnydale and this general vicinity."

"Well, he's gone now. Good riddance. He was a terrible customer."

"The sheriff's deputies think he's still in the area. So they have all the roads out of town blocked off and are checking each car as it goes through. But they haven't found him yet. So, where do you think he went after eating here?"

"I am not sure. I never saw him leave." Mary suddenly felt sick to her stomach.

"You didn't?"

"No, I didn't. Do you think he's still in the diner?"

"You and Eddy, leave now, out the front door."

"I'm not going to leave you alone."

"Mary, go now. This is my job. I am not going to put you in danger."

"You should have listened to your brother, Mary, and left when you had the chance." The rude customer came out of the back room with his gun drawn, pointing at them.

"Let them go, John Olander."

"Oh, so you know who I am. I think they will make wonderful hostages. Thank you for letting me know that all the roads are blocked getting out of town. With Mary and Eddy in my car, they will have to let me pass."

"I will never let you take them."

"Well, you won't have a choice."

John walked up to Frank and hit him over the head with his gun—he dropped to the ground with a sickening thud, and Mary screamed.

"Don't do that again!" the criminal yelled.

Mary ignored him, dropped to the ground, and took care of Frank. She held two fingers to his neck to see if he was still alive. Mary sighed with relief when she felt a pulse.

"Let's go, Mary. I figure I only need one of you to make my escape."

John stepped toward Mary. Eddy was on the other side of the room and flung himself at John, flipping him to the ground and knocking the gun out of his hand. It hit the floor

with a loud clang, and Mary moved to get it. Unfortunately, Eddy and John were still wrestling and didn't realize Mary held the gun pointed at them.

"Eddy, get out of the way!" Mary screamed.

John tried to hold Eddy in place, but he escaped his grasp and went to stand by Mary.

"Wow, I'm impressed. Maybe you should have been the one to attend the police academy," Frank said, rubbing his head. He went over to John on the floor and handcuffed him.

"You are under arrest."

"Oh my gosh, Frank, are you okay?" Mary was on the verge of tears.

"Thanks to you, Mary, I am fine." Frank went over and gave her a big hug and took the gun out of her hand. "I love you, Sis."

"I love you too, Mary," Eddy said from behind her.

"What did you say?"

"I said I love you too. It was me that has been giving you the notes. I thought you would like a buildup."

"A buildup to what?"

Eddy dropped to one knee and grabbed Mary's hand.

"Mary Allison, I have loved you my whole life. Will you marry me?"

"I-I-I," Mary stuttered.

"I what, Mary?"

"I'd be honored, Eddy."

Eddy and Mary kissed until her brother cleared his throat.

"As romantic as that was, this is still a crime scene. I will need to call the Landsberg Police Department, so this place will be getting very busy. Do you think you could hold off on the kissy face for a while?"

"Oh, shut up, sergeant bossy pants." Mary stuck her tongue out at him.

"I will move John to my squad car and call in backup. Congratulations, you two, this has to be the weirdest proposal ever," Frank said as he walked the criminal out the door.

"Thank you so much for saving my life, Eddy. I love you."

"I love you too, Mary." He reached out for her hand and held it for a moment. "And I know for a fact that the new owner of the diner is not a jerk."

"How do you know that?"

"Because we are the new owners."

ABOUT THE AUTHOR

Ann Aubitz is the Co-owner and Publisher of Kirk House Publishers and FuzionPress, located in Burnsville, Minnesota. After years of reading everything she could get her hands on, she decided to help others achieve their dream of becoming an author. Her mission is to help authors reach their goals by seeing their books in print.

Ann is also a proud member of the Independent Book Publishers Association, a Board Member-At-Large for the Midwest Independent Publishers Association, and a group leader for Women of Words and chairs the yearly WOW writing conference.

STORY TEN

Wow, Bowling?

By Ava Florian Johns

"Robert, where are we going?"

"I told you, Patty, we're going to the bowling alley to meet up with my friends."

"Some date this is turning out to be. And I told you to call me Patricia."

"Why?" Robert shook his head. Patty had been his friend since they were babies. They lived next to each other their whole lives, but lately, he felt like he didn't know her.

"Because I am going for a more sophisticated sound, and I am almost eighteen. Patty is a little girl's name." She huffed, then continued, "So why are we seeing your friends again?

"Because I thought it would be fun. You like my friends, don't you?"

"Yeah, but didn't you say this was a date?" Patricia bent down to fix her bobby socks.

"Well, ya, but can't it be a date with my friends?"

"Um, no. If I had known this wasn't an actual date, I'd have gone to the diner and the drive-in with my friends. There's a double feature at the drive-in tonight, *Gidget* and *The Shaggy Dog*."

"Sounds pretty boring to me," Robert said, yawning.

"Not as boring as bowling with your friends." Patty gave him a fake yawn back.

Robert thought for a minute. "How about we get our own lane?"

"That's a start. You can also get me the french fries that I like too."

"Anything else?"

"Nope, that'll do it." Robert shook his head again. Patty was a handful, but she was the only girl he could really talk to. He knew that she wanted romance, but he didn't' know how to do that.

Robert parked the car and went around the side to open Patty's door.

"Nice. Thank you."

"See, I'm really trying here, Patty. I mean Patricia."

Patty smiled and held out her hand so he could help her out of the car. They both knew this wasn't necessary; she was perfectly capable of getting herself out of the car, but it was nice to hold Robert's hand. In all the years they had known each other, the most romantic that they got was holding

hands. Patty was hoping that tonight's 'date' would change that. She had been practicing her good night kiss all day. So it was like dousing a flame with icy water when he told her they were going bowling.

He held her hand as they walked up to the door. The new song "Venus" by Frankie Avalon was pouring out the door into the night as soon as they opened it. Robert smiled. Patty loved Frankie Avalon. Robert thought maybe this date wasn't going so bad after all.

Patty knew she was giving Robert a tough time about going to the bowling alley, but truthfully, she loved it. The jukebox always had the latest hits. They had a big hula hoop contest on Saturday nights, and the bowling alley kitchen had the best fries and malts in town. She wasn't unhappy about being at the bowling alley, she just thought Robert was starting to see her as more than just a friend, but maybe she was wrong. She really liked him. He was the only boy she ever wanted, and he put up with her crazy stunts. All through their childhood, she cooked up wacky schemes, and he went along with them. She often said she was the brains of the operation, and he was the muscle.

They went to the counter to get their bowling shoes, and sure enough, all of Robert's friends came over to say hi and impress Robert with stories of their bowling triumph over the other local bowling team.

Patty was only half-listening. It turned out the same wherever they went together. Robert's friends would descend on them, and they wouldn't get any time alone. The thing that bothered her most was that he didn't seem to mind. His mother always said he would go into public office to be the mayor because everyone gravitated toward him.

"Robert, while you're talking to your friends, I'll go order our french fries and malts, okay?"

"No, Patty, I'll go with you." He put his arm around Patty's shoulder and led her toward the food counter. "See you later, boys."

"Aw, come on, Robert, we need you for the next game."

"No can do, boys, I'm with my girl tonight." Robert smiled and held her tighter.

"Thanks, Robert." Patty smiled up at him.

"No problem, Patricia. I'm sorry this date isn't what you expected."

"That's okay—it's not so bad. And you can call me Patty. I like when you say it."

"Okay, Patty."

Suddenly, there was a commotion at the other end of the bowling alley. A group of local boys were causing trouble with

the waitress. They were knocking stuff out of her hands to the floor and generally acting like brutes. While this was taking place, Mr. Olson, who owned the bowling alley, came toward Robert and Patty.

"Someone broke into my office and stole the money from yesterday's till. I didn't have time to bring the money to the bank today. Robert, I saw one of your friends over by my office door a few minutes ago."

"One of my friends? Which one?"

"That little one, Freddie." Patty was shaking her head no as Mr. Olson was speaking. She knew there was no way that it was Robert's group of friends. Actually, she should say *her* group of friends. She had known them as long or longer than Robert.

"Freddie would never steal money or anything. He is not like that." Patty said.

"Well, I heard he lived in one of those boys' homes." Mr. Olson said with a look of disgust on his face.

"Not because he's trouble, but because he doesn't have parents. He's a great kid." Robert continued to stick up for Freddie.

"Well, whatever the reason, he was the one that I saw by the door." Mr. Olson started walking away.

"Fine, I'll talk to him, but I wouldn't rule out other people in the bowling alley. I think you should lock the doors, call the police, and make an announcement over the loudspeaker. If

the person gets out the doors with your money, it is long gone."

"Good Idea. Thanks, Robert."

Patty loved the way everyone came to Robert for advice. She thought back to what his mom said about him being mayor. He would be terrific.

Patty and Robert walked over to where their friends were standing.

"Freddie, I need to talk to you a minute." Robert walked up to the group and put his arm around Freddie.

"What's up, daddio?"

"Mr. Olson told us you stole money from his office." Robert hated to be the one to accuse him.

Freddie and the boys looked shocked. Robert knew at that moment that Freddie didn't steal the money. As Robert was handling the issues and talking to his friends, Patty looked at all the colorful bowling balls on the racks. She loved to look at the shiny colorful swirls on the bowling balls. She picked up a pink one to see if it was suitable for her. At that same time, she heard screaming from the doorway. The owner, Mr. Olson, was trying to lock the door, and the neighborhood hooligans were trying to get out.

"I'm sorry, but no one can leave until I figure out who stole the money. I was just about to announce that everyone needs to sit down while we search the bowling alley."

"You can't do that; I know my rights."

"We have called the police, Mr. Flannigan, and they will be here in a minute. You can voice your grievance to them."

Patty still holding the bowling ball inched closer to the door where the fight was taking place. Robert was still engrossed in the conversation with Freddie. Patty knew Mr. Flannigan quite well. His name was Thad, and her mom babysat him until he turned about seven and became too wild for her. Thad was always bullying Patty and never let her play with the toys she wanted. Instead, he would take them and hold them over her head so she couldn't reach them. So basically, he was a big jerk—and judging by his behavior tonight, he hadn't changed a bit.

"Mr. Flannigan, I will ask you again. Please take a seat."

"No way, we're leaving." Thad had his gang lined up behind him, trying to intimidate poor Mr. Olson.

"I'm afraid I can't let you do that." Mr. Olson stood his ground.

"Well, I wasn't asking you, was I? Boys, let's go." Thad knocked Mr. Olson to the floor.

Patty gasped, drawing his attention to her. She had inched so close that they were only about ten feet apart.

"Oh, if it isn't little Pattycake."

"Don't call me that, Thaddeus."

"Oooo," his friends mocked.

"You never were too bright." Thad started moving toward her.

"Neither were you, Thaddeus." Patty took the bowling ball in her hand and rolled it as hard as she could directly toward him. The look of surprise on his face told her that he hadn't expected that she would do something like that.

The bowling ball hit his legs and Thaddeus fell to the floor just as the police busted through the doors. Patty ran over the floor to see if Mr. Olson was okay.

"I guess he was bowled over." Mr. Olson laughed at his own joke.

"How are you, Mr. Olson?" Patty looked worried.

"Oh honey, I am okay, thanks to you."

While Patty was talking to Mr. Olson. The police searched Thaddeus and his group of hooligans for the missing cash, and they found some of the stolen money on each of the five guys in Thad's group. While the guys were causing a scene with the waitress, Thaddeus had snuck into the back office and took the money from Mr. Olson's desk.

Robert ran over to Patty.

"I know what you are going to say—I shouldn't have done it. It was dangerous."

"It was dangerous, but that isn't what I was going to say." Robert moved toward her.

"What..." Before Patty could finish her sentence Robert kissed her on the lips. Then she exclaimed, "Wow, Bowling!"

ABOUT THE AUTHOR

Ava Florian Johns writes in the science fiction genre. Her characters are clever and fearless, but in real life, Ava is afraid of her basement, bees, and especially clowns. Truth be told Ava wouldn't last five minutes in one of her books.

Ava is best known for her *Omega Team Series*.

CONCLUSION

Thank you for reading Reminisce Mysteries. We hope you enjoyed the stories.

Watch for the next books in our the Reminisce series to be released. They will be announced on our website. www.kirkhousepublishers.com

Reminisce Romance—Book Two

Reminisce Ghost Stories—Book Three

Reminisce Science Fiction—Book Four